CW01506583

MURDER
IN
WINTERTIME

ALSO AVAILABLE

Murder Takes a Holiday
Murder by the Seaside
Murder in Midsummer
Murder in a Heatwave
Murder Under the Sun
Murder at the Beach

Murder Under the Christmas Tree
Murder on Christmas Eve
A Very Murderous Christmas
Murder at Christmas
Murder in Midwinter
Murder on a Winter's Night
Murder in the Falling Snow
The Dead of Winter
Murder by Candlelight

MURDER IN WINTERTIME

CLASSIC CRIME STORIES

Edited by Cecily Gayford

Peter Lovesey · Carter Dickson · P.D. James
Edmund Crispin · Catherine Aird · Will Scott
Colin Dexter · William Bankier
Arthur Conan Doyle

Profile Books

First published in Great Britain in 2025 by
PROFILE BOOKS LTD
29 Cloth Fair
London ECIA 7JQ
www.profilebooks.com

Selection copyright © Cecily Gayford, 2025
See p. 247 for individual stories' copyright information

1 3 5 7 9 10 8 6 4 2

Typeset in Fournier by MacGuru Ltd
Printed and bound in Great Britain by
CPI Group (UK) Ltd, Croydon CRO 4YY

The moral rights of the authors has been asserted.

All rights reserved. Without limiting the rights under copyright
reserved above, no part of this publication may be reproduced,
stored or introduced into a retrieval system, or transmitted, in
any form or by any means (electronic, mechanical, photocopying,
recording or otherwise), without the prior written permission of
both the copyright owner and the publisher of this book.

A CIP catalogue record for this book is available from the British Library.

Our product safety representative in the EU is Authorised
Rep Compliance Ltd., Ground Floor, 71 Lower Baggot Street,
Dublin, DO2 P593, Ireland. www.arccompliance.com

ISBN 978 1 80522 499 0
eISBN 978 1 80522 5003

Contents

The Haunted Crescent

Peter Lovesey

A ghost was seen last Christmas in a certain house in the Royal Crescent. Believe me, this is true. I speak from personal experience, as a resident of the City of Bath and something of an authority on psychic phenomena. I readily admit that ninety-nine per cent of so-called hauntings turn out to have been hallucinations of one sort or another, but this is the exception, a genuine haunted house. Out of consideration for the present owners (who for obvious reasons wish to preserve their privacy), I shall not disclose the exact address, but if you doubt me, read what happened to me on Christmas Eve, 1988.

The couple who own the house had gone to Norfolk for the festive season, leaving on Friday, December twenty-third. Good planning. The ghost was reputed to walk on Christmas Eve. Knowing of my interest, they had generously placed their house at my disposal. I am an ex-policeman, by the way, and it takes a lot to frighten me.

For those who like a ghost story with all the trimmings – deep snow and howling winds outside – I am sorry. I must disappoint you. Christmas, 1988, was not a white one in Bath. It was unseasonably warm. There wasn't even any fog. All I can offer in the way of atmospheric effects are a full moon that night and an owl that hooted periodically in the trees at the far side of the sloping lawn that fronts the Crescent. It has to be admitted that this was not a spooky-looking barn owl, but a tawny owl, which on this night was making more of a high-pitched 'kee-wik' call than a hoot, quite cheery, in fact. Do not despair, however.

The things that happened in the house that night more than compensated for the absence of werewolves and banshees outside.

It is vital to the story that you are sufficiently informed about the building in which the events occurred. Whether you realise it or not, you have probably seen the Royal Crescent, if not as a resident, or a tourist, then in one of the numerous films in which it has appeared as a backdrop to the action. It is in a quiet location north-west of the city and comprises thirty houses in a semi-elliptical terrace completed in 1774 to the specification of John Wood the Younger. It stands comparison with any domestic building in Europe. I defy anyone not to respond to its uncomplicated grandeur, the majestic panorama of 114 Ionic columns topped by a portico and balustrade; and the roadway at the front where Jane Austen and Charles Dickens trod the cobbles. But you want me to come to the ghost.

My first intimation of something unaccountable came

at about twenty past eleven that Christmas Eve. I was in the drawing room on the first floor. I had stationed myself there a couple of hours before. The door was ajar and the house was in darkness. No, that isn't quite accurate. I should have said simply that none of the lights were switched on; actually the moonlight gave a certain amount of illumination, silver-blue rectangles projected across the carpet and over the base of the Christmas tree, producing an effect infinitely prettier than fairy lights. The furniture was easily visible, too, armchairs, table and grand piano. One's eyes adjust. It didn't strike me as eerie to be alone in that unlit house. Anyone knows that a spirit of the departed is unlikely to manifest itself in electric light.

No house is totally silent, certainly no centrally heated house. The sounds produced by expanding floorboards in so-called haunted houses up and down the land must have fooled ghost-hunters by the hundred. In this case, as a precaution against a sudden freeze, the owners had left the system switched on. It was timed to turn off at eleven, so the knocks and creaks I was hearing now ought to have been the last of the night.

As events turned out, it wasn't a sound that alerted me first. It was a sudden draft against my face and a flutter of white across the room. I tensed. The house had gone silent. I crossed the room to investigate.

The disturbance had been caused by a Christmas card falling off the mantelpiece into the grate. Nothing more alarming than that. Cards are always falling down. That's why some people prefer to suspend them on strings. I stooped, picked up the card, and replaced it, smiling at my overactive imagination.

Yet I had definitely noticed a draft. The house was supposed to be free of drafts. All the doors and windows were closed and meticulously sealed against the elements. Strange. I listened, holding my breath. The drawing room where I was standing was well placed for picking up any unexplained sound in the house. It was at the centre of the building. Below me were the ground floor and the cellar, above me the second floor and the attic.

Hearing nothing, I decided to venture out to the landing and listen there. I was mystified, yet unwilling at this stage to countenance a supernatural explanation. I was inclined to wonder whether the cut-off of the central heating had resulted in some trick of convection that gave the impression or the reality of a disturbance in the air. The falling card was not significant in itself. The draft required an explanation. My state of mind, you see, was calm and analytical.

Ten or fifteen seconds passed. I leaned over the banisters and looked down the stairwell to make sure that the front door was firmly shut, and so it proved to be. Then I heard a rustle from the room where I had been. I knew what it was – the card falling into the grate again – for another distinct movement of air had stirred the curtain on the landing window, causing a shift in the moonlight across the stairs. I was in no doubt anymore that this was worth investigating. My only uncertainty was whether to start with the floors above me, or below.

I chose the latter, reasoning that if, as I suspected, someone had opened a window, it was likely to be at the ground or basement levels. My assumption was wrong. I shall not draw out the suspense. I merely wish to record that I checked the cellar, kitchen, scullery, dining room and study and found every window and external door secure and bolted from inside. No one could have entered after me.

So I began to work my way upstairs again, methodically visiting each room. And on the staircase to the second floor, I heard a sigh.

Occasionally in Victorian novels a character would 'heave' a sigh. Somehow the phrase had always irritated me. In real life I never heard a sigh so weighty that it seemed to involve muscular effort – until this moment. This was a sound hauled up from the depths of somebody's inner being, or so I deduced. Whether it really originated with somebody or some *thing* was open to speculation.

The sound had definitely come from above me. Unable by now to suppress my excitement, I moved up to the second-floor landing, where I found three doors, all closed. I moved from one to the other, opening them rapidly and glancing briefly inside. Two bedrooms and a bathroom. I hesitated. A bathroom. Had the 'sigh', I wondered, been caused by some aberration of the plumbing? Air locks are endemic in the complicated systems installed in these old Georgian buildings. The houses were not built with valves and cisterns. The efficiency of the pipework depended on the variable skill of generations of plumbers.

The sound must have been caused by trapped air.

Rationality reasserted itself. I would finish my inspection and prove to my total satisfaction that what I had heard was neither human nor spectral in origin. I closed the bathroom door behind me and crossed the landing to the last flight of stairs, more narrow than those I had used so far. In times past they had been the means of access to the servants' quarters in the attic. I glanced up at the white-painted door at the head of these stairs and observed that it was slightly ajar.

My foot was on the first stair and my hand on the rail when I stiffened. That door moved.

It was being drawn inward. The movement was slow and deliberate. As the gap increased, a faint glow of moonlight was cast from the interior onto the panelling to my right. I stared up and watched the figure of a woman appear in the doorway.

She was in a white gown or robe that reached to her feet. Her hair hung loose to the level of her chest – fine, gently shifting hair so pale in colour that it appeared to merge with the dress. Her skin, too, appeared bloodless. The eyes were flint black, however. They widened as they took me in. Her right hand crept to her throat and I heard her give a gasp.

The sensations I experienced in that moment of confrontation are difficult to convey. I was convinced that nothing of flesh and blood had entered that house in the hours I had been there. All the entrances were bolted – I had checked. I could not account for the phenomenon, or whatever it was, that had manifested itself, yet I refused to be convinced. I was unwilling to accept what my eyes were seeing and my rational faculties could not explain. She could not be a ghost.

I said, 'Who are you?'

The figure swayed back as if startled. For a moment I thought she was going to close the attic door, but she remained staring at me, her hand still pressed to her throat. It was the face and form of a young woman, not more than twenty.

I asked, 'Can you speak?'

She appeared to nod.

I said, 'What are you doing here?'

She caught her breath. In a strange, half-whispered utterance she said, as if echoing my words, 'Who are you?'

I took a step upward towards her. It evidently frightened her, for she backed away and became almost invisible in the shadowy interior of the attic room. I tried to dredge up some reassuring words. 'It's all right. Believe me, it's all right.'

Then I twitched in surprise. Downstairs, the doorbell chimed. After eleven on Christmas Eve!

I said, 'What on earth …?'

The woman in white whimpered something I couldn't hear.

I tried to make light of it. 'Santa, I expect.'

She didn't react.

The bell rang a second time.

'He ought to be using the chimney,' I said. I had already decided to ignore the visitor, whoever it was. One unexpected caller was all I could cope with.

The young woman spoke up, and the words sprang clearly from her. 'For God's sake, send him away!'

'You know who it is?'

'Please! I beg you.'

'If you know who it is,' I said reasonably, 'wouldn't you like to answer it?'

'I can't.'

The chimes rang out again.

I said, 'Is it someone you know?'

'Please. Tell him to go away. If you answer the door he'll go away.'

I was letting myself be persuaded. I needed her cooperation. I wanted to know about her. 'All right,' I relented. 'But will you be here when I come back?'

'I won't leave.'

Instinctively I trusted her. I turned and descended the two flights of stairs to the hall. The bell rang again. Even though the house was in darkness, the caller had no intention of giving up.

I drew back the bolts, opened the front door a fraction, and looked out. A man was on the doorstep, leaning on the iron railing. A young man in a leather jacket glittering with studs and chains. His head was shaven. He, at any rate, looked like flesh and blood. He said, 'What kept you?'

I said, 'What do you want?'

He glared. 'For crying out loud – who the hell are you?' His eyes slid sideways, checking the number on the wall.

I said with frigid courtesy, 'I think you must have made a mistake.'

'No,' he said. 'This is the house all right. What's your game, mate? What are you doing here with the lights off?'

I told him that I was an observer of psychic phenomena.

'Come again?'

'Ghosts,' I said. 'This house has the reputation of being haunted. The owners have kindly allowed me to keep watch tonight.'

'Oh, yes?' he said with heavy scepticism. 'Spooks, is it? I'll have a gander at them meself.' With that, he gave the door a shove. There was no security chain and I was unable to resist the pressure. He stepped across the threshold. 'Ghostbuster, are you, mate? You wouldn't, by any chance, be lifting the family silver at the same time? Anyone else in here?'

I said, 'I take exception to that. You've no right to force your way in here.'

'No more right than you,' he said, stepping past me. 'Were you upstairs when I rang?'

I said, 'I'm going to call the police.'

He flapped his hand dismissively. 'Be my guest. I'm going upstairs, right?'

Sheer panic inspired me to say, 'If you do, you'll be on film.'

'What?'

'The cameras are ready to roll,' I lied. 'The place is riddled with mikes and tripwires.'

He said, 'I don't believe you,' but the tone of his voice said the opposite.

'This ghost is supposed to walk on Christmas Eve,' I told him. 'I want to capture it on film.' I gave a special resonance to the word 'capture'.

He said, 'You're round the twist.' And with as much dignity as he could muster he sidled back towards the door, which still stood open. Apparently he was leaving. 'You ought to be locked up. You're a nutcase.'

As he stepped out of the door I said, 'Shall I tell the owners you called? What name shall I give?'

He swore and turned away. I closed the door and slid the bolts back into place. I was shaking. It had been an ugly, potentially dangerous incident. I'm not so capable of tackling an intruder as I once was and I was thankful that my powers of invention had served me so well.

I started up the stairs again and as I reached the top of the first flight, the young woman in white was waiting for me. She must have come down two floors to overhear what was being said. This area of the house was better illuminated than the attic stairs, so I got a better look at her. She appeared less ethereal now. Her dress was silk or satin, I observed. It was an evening gown. Her make-up was as pale as a mime artist's, except for the black liner around her eyes.

She said, 'How can I thank you enough?'

I answered flatly, 'What I want from you, young lady, is an explanation.'

She crossed her arms, rubbing at her sleeves. 'I feel shivery here. Do you mind if we go in there?'

As we moved into the drawing room I noticed that she made no attempt to switch on the light. She pointed to some cigarettes on the table. 'Do you mind?'

I found some matches by the fireplace and gave her a light. 'Who was that at the door?'

She inhaled hard. 'Some guy I met at a party. I was supposed to be with someone else, but we got separated. You know how it is. Next thing I knew, this bloke in the leather jacket was chatting me up. He was all right at first. I didn't know he was going to come on so strong. I mean I didn't encourage him. I was trying to cool it. He offered me these tablets, but I refused. He said they would make me relax. By then I was really scared. I moved off fast. The stupid thing was that I moved upstairs. There were plenty of people about, and it seemed the easiest way to go. The bloke followed. He kept on following. I went right to the top of the house and shut myself in a room. I pushed a cupboard against the door.

He was beating his fist on the door, saying what he was going to do to me. I was scared out of my skull. All I could think of doing was get through the window, so I did. I climbed out and found myself up there behind the little stone wall.'

'Of this building? The balustrade at the top?'

'Didn't I make that clear? The party was in a house a couple of doors away from you. I ran along this narrow passageway between the roof and the wall, trying all the windows. The one upstairs was the first one I could shift.'

'The attic window. Now I understand.' The sudden draft was explained, and the gasp as she had caught her breath after the effort.

She said, 'I'm really grateful.'

'Grateful?'

'Grateful to you for getting rid of him.'

I said, 'It would be sensible now to call a taxi. Where do you live?'

'Not far. I can walk.'

'It wouldn't be advisable, would it, after what happened? He's persistent. He may be waiting.'

'I didn't think.' She stubbed the cigarette into an ashtray. After a moment's reflection she said, 'All right. Where's the phone?'

There was one in the study. While she was occupied, I gave some thought to what she had said. I didn't believe a word of it, but I had something vastly more important on my mind.

She came back into the room. 'Ten minutes, they reckon. Was it true what you said downstairs, about this house being haunted?'

'Mm?' I was still preoccupied.

'The spook. All that stuff about hidden cameras. Did you mean it?'

'There aren't any cameras. I'm useless with machinery of any sort. I reckoned he'd think twice about coming in if he knew he was going to be on film. It was just a bluff.'

'And the bit about the ghost?'

'That was true.'

'Would you mind telling me about it?'

'Aren't you afraid of the supernatural?'

'It's scary, yes. Not so scary as what happened already. I want to know the story. Christmas Eve is a great night for a ghost story.'

I said, 'It's more than just a story.'

'Please.'

'On one condition. Before you get into that taxi, you tell me the truth about yourself – why you really came into this house tonight.'

She hesitated.

I said, 'It needn't go any further.'

'All right. Tell me about the ghost.' She reached for another cigarette and perched on the arm of a chair.

I crossed to the window and looked away over the lawn towards the trees silhouetted against the city lights. 'It can be traced back, as all ghost stories can, to a story of death and an unquiet spirit. About a hundred and fifty years ago this house was owned by an army officer, a retired colonel by the name of Davenport. He had a daughter called Rosamund, and it was believed in the city that he doted on her. She was dressed fashionably and given a good education, which in those days was beyond the expectation of most young women. Rosamund was a lively, intelligent and attractive girl. Her hair when she wore it long was very like yours, fine and extremely fair. Not surprisingly, she had admirers. The one she favoured most was a young man from Bristol, Luke Robertson, who at that time was an architect. In the conventions of the time they formed an attachment which amounted to little more than a few chaperoned meetings, some letters, poems, and so on. They were lovers in a very old-fashioned sense that you may find difficult to credit. In physical terms it amounted to no more than a few stolen kisses, if that. Somewhere in this house there is supposed to be carved into woodwork the letters *L* and *R* linked. I can't show you. I haven't found it.'

Outside, a taxi trundled over the cobbles. I watched it draw up at a house some doors down. Two couples came out of the building, laughing, and climbed into the cab. It was obvious that they were leaving a party. The heavy beat of music carried up to me.

I said, 'I wonder if it's turned midnight. It might be Christmas Day already.'

She said, 'Please go on with the story.'

'Colonel Davenport – the father of this girl – was a lonely man. His wife had died some years before. Lately he had become friendly with a neighbour, another resident of the Crescent, a widow approaching fifty years of age by the name of Mrs Crandley, who lived in one of the houses at the far end of the building. She was a musician, a pianist, and she gave lessons. One of her pupils was Rosamund. So far as one can tell, Mrs Crandley was a good teacher and the girl a promising pupil. Do you play?'

'What?'

I turned to face her. 'I said, do you play the piano?'

'Oh. Just a bit,' said the girl.

'You didn't tell me your name.'

'I'd rather not, if you don't mind. What happened between the colonel and Mrs Crandley?'

'Their friendship blossomed. He wanted her to marry him. Mrs Crandley was not unwilling. In fact, she agreed, subject to one condition. She had a son of twenty-seven called Justinian.'

'What was that?'

'Justinian. There was a vogue for calling your children after emperors. This Justinian was a dull fellow without much to recommend him. He was lazy and overweight. He rarely ventured out of the house. Mrs Crandley despaired of him.'

'She wanted him off her hands?'

'That is what it amounted to. She wanted him married and she saw the perfect partner for him in Rosamund. Surely such a charming, talented girl would bring out some positive qualities in her lumpish son. Mrs Crandley applied herself diligently to the plan, insisting that Justinian answer the doorbell each time Rosamund came for her music lesson. Then he would be told to sit in the room and listen to her playing. Everything Mrs Crandley could do to promote the match was done. For his part, Justinian was content to go along with the plan. He was promised that if he married the girl he would be given his mother's house, so the pattern of his life would alter little, except that a pretty wife would keep him company rather than a discontented, nagging mother.

He began to eye Rosamund with increasing favour. So when the colonel proposed marriage to Mrs Crandley, she assented on the understanding that Justinian would be married to Rosamund at the same time.'

'How about Rosamund? Was she given any choice?'

'You have to be aware that marriages were commonly arranged by the parents in those days.'

'But you said she already had a lover. He was perfectly respectable, wasn't he?'

I nodded. 'Absolutely. But Luke Robertson didn't feature in Mrs Crandley's plan. He was ignored. Rosamund bowed under the pressure and became engaged to Justinian in the autumn of 1838. The double marriage was to take place in the Abbey on Christmas Eve.'

'Oh, dear – I think I can guess the rest of the story.'

'It may not be quite as you expect. As the day of the wedding approached, Rosamund began to dread the prospect. She pleaded with her father to allow her to break off the engagement. He wouldn't hear of it. He loved Mrs Crandley and his thoughts were all of her. In despair, Rosamund sent the maidservant with a message to Luke, asking him to meet her secretly on the basement steps. She had a romantic notion that Luke would elope with her.'

My listener was enthralled. 'And did he come?'

'He came. Rosamund poured out her story. Luke listened with sympathy, but he was cautious. He didn't see elopement as the solution. Rather bravely, he volunteered to speak to the colonel and appeal to him to allow Rosamund to marry the man of her choice. If that failed, he would remind the colonel that Rosamund could not be forced to take the sacred vows. Her consent had to be freely given in church, and she was entitled to withhold it. So this uncomfortable interview took place a day or two later. The colonel, naturally, was outraged. Luke was banished from the house and forbidden to speak to Rosamund again. The unfortunate girl was summoned by her father and accused of wickedly consorting with her former lover when she was promised to another. The story of the secret note and the meeting on the stairs was dragged from her. She was told that she wished to destroy her father's marriage. She was said to be selfish and disloyal. Worse, she might be taken to court by Justinian for breach of promise.'

'Poor little soul! Did it break her?'

'No. Amazingly, she stood her ground. Luke's support had given her courage. She would not marry Justinian. It was the colonel who backed down. He went to see Mrs Crandley. When he returned, it was to tell Rosamund that his marriage would not, after all, take place. Mrs Crandley had insisted on a double wedding, or nothing.'

'I wouldn't have been in Rosamund's shoes for a million pounds.'

'She was told by her father that she had behaved no better than a servant, secretly meeting her lover on the basement steps and trifling with another man's affections, so in future he would treat her as a servant. And he did. He dismissed the housemaid. He ordered Rosamund to move her things to the maid's room in the attic, and he gave her a list of duties that kept her busy from five-thirty each morning until late at night.'

'Cruel.'

'All his bitterness was heaped on her.'

'Did she kill herself?'

'No,' I said with only the slightest pause. 'She was murdered.'

'*Murdered?*'

'On Christmas Eve, the day that the weddings would have taken place, she was suffocated in her bed.'

'Horrible!'

'A pillow was held against her face until she ceased to breathe. She was found dead in bed by the cook on Christmas morning after she failed to report for duty. The colonel was informed and the police were sent for.'

'Who killed her?'

'The inspector on the case, a local man without much experience of violent crimes, was in no doubt that Colonel Davenport was the murderer. He had a powerful motive. The animus he felt towards his daughter had been demonstrated by the way he treated her. It seemed that his anger had only increased as the days passed. On the date he was due to have married, it became insupportable.'

'Was it true? Did he confess to killing her?'

'He refused to make any statement. But the evidence against him was overwhelming. Three inches of snow fell on Christmas Eve. It stopped about eight-thirty that evening. The time of death was estimated at about eleven p.m. When the inspector and his men arrived next morning no footsteps were visible on the path leading to the front door except those of the cook, who had gone for the police. The only other person in the house was Colonel Davenport. So he was charged with murdering his own daughter. The trial was short, for he refused to plead. He remained silent to the end. He was found guilty and hanged at Bristol in February 1839.'

She put out the cigarette. 'Grim.'

'Yes.'

'There's more to the story, isn't there? The ghost. You said something about an unquiet spirit.'

I said, 'There was a feeling of unease about the fact that the colonel wouldn't admit to the crime. After he was convicted and condemned, they tried to persuade him to confess, to lay his sins before his Maker. A murderer often would confess in the last days remaining to him, even after protesting innocence all through the trial. They all did their utmost to persuade him – the prison governor, the warders, the priest, and the hangman himself. Those people had harrowing duties to perform. It would have helped them to know that the man going to the gallows was truly guilty of the crime. Not one word would that proud old man speak.'

'You sound almost sorry for him. There wasn't really any doubt, was there?'

I said, 'There's a continuous history of supernatural happenings in this house for a century and a half. Think about it. Suppose, for example, someone else committed the murder.'

'But who else could have?'

'Justinian Crandley.'

'That's impossible. He didn't live here. His footprints would have shown up in the snow.'

'Not if he entered the house as you did tonight – along the roof and through the attic window. He could have murdered Rosamund and returned to his own house by the same route.'

'It's possible, I suppose, but why – what was his motive?'

'Revenge. He would have been master in his own house if the marriage had not been called off. Instead, he faced an indefinite future with his domineering and now embittered mother. He blamed Rosamund. He decided that if he was not to have her as his wife, no one else should.'

'Is that what you believe?'

'It is now,' said I.

'Why didn't the colonel tell them he was innocent?'

'He blamed himself. He felt a deep sense of guilt for the way he had treated his own daughter. But for his selfishness the murder would never have taken place.'

'Do you think he knew the truth?'

'He must have worked it out. He loved Mrs Crandley too much to cause her further unhappiness.'

There was an interval of silence, broken finally by the sound of car tyres on the cobbles below.

She stood up. 'Tonight when you saw me at the attic door you thought I was Rosamund's ghost.'

I said, 'No. Rosamund doesn't haunt this place. Her spirit is at rest. I didn't take you for a real ghost any more than I believed your story of escaping from the fellow in the leather jacket.'

She walked to the window. 'It is my taxi.'

I wasn't going to let her leave without admitting the truth. 'You went to the party two doors along with the idea of breaking into this house. You climbed out onto the roof and forced your way in upstairs, meaning to let your friend in by the front door. You were going to burgle the place.'

She gasped and swung around. 'How did you know that?'

'When I opened the door he was expecting you. He said

19

"What kept you?" He knew which house to call at, so it must have been planned. If your story had been true, he wouldn't have known where to come.'

She stared down at the waiting cab.

I said, 'Until I suggested the taxi, you were quite prepared to go out into the street where this man who had allegedly threatened you was waiting.'

'I'm leaving.'

'And I noticed that you didn't want the lights turned on.'

Her tone altered. 'You're not one of the fuzz, are you? You wouldn't turn me in? Give me a break, will you? It's the first time. I'll never try it again.'

'How can I know that?'

'I'll give you my name and address, if you want. Then you can check.'

It is sufficient to state here that she supplied the information. I shall keep it to myself. I'm no longer in the business of exposing petty criminals. I saw her to her taxi. She promised to stop seeing her boyfriend. Perhaps you think I let her off too lightly. Her misdemeanour was minor compared with the discovery I had made – and I owed that discovery to her.

It released me from my obligation, you see. I told you I was once a policeman. An inspector, actually. I made a fatal mistake. I have had a hundred and fifty years to search for the truth and now that I have found it I can rest. The haunting of the Royal Crescent is at an end.

New Murders for Old

Carter Dickson

Hargreaves did not speak until he had turned on two lamps. Even then he did not remove his overcoat. The room, though cold, was stuffy, and held a faintly sweet odour. Outside the Venetian blinds, which were not quite closed, you saw the restless, shifting presence of snow past street lights. For the first time, Hargreaves hesitated.

'The – the object,' he explained, indicating the bed, 'was there. *He* came in by this door, here. Perhaps you understand a little better now?'

Hargreaves' companion nodded.

'No,' said Hargreaves, and smiled. 'I'm not trying to invoke illusions. On the contrary, I am trying to dispel them. Shall we go downstairs?'

It was a tall, heavy house, where no clocks ticked. But the treads of the stairs creaked and cracked sharply, even under their padding of carpet. At the back, in a kind of small study, a gas fire had been lighted. Its hissing could be heard from a distance; it roared up blue, like solid blue flames, into the white fretwork of the heater; but it did little to dispel the chill of the room. Hargreaves motioned his companion to a chair at the other side of the fire.

'I want to tell you about it,' he went on. 'Don't think I'm trying to be—' his wrist hesitated over a word, as though over a chess piece – 'highbrow. Don't think I'm trying to be highbrow if I tell it to you' – again his wrist hesitated – 'objectively. As though you knew nothing about it. As though you weren't concerned in it. It's the only way you will understand the problem he had to face.'

Hargreaves was very intent when he said this. He was bending forward, looking up from under his eyebrows; his heavy overcoat flopped over the sides of his knees, and his gloved hands, seldom still, either made a slight gesture or pressed flat on his knees.

'Take Tony Marvell, to begin with,' he argued. 'A good fellow, whom everybody liked. Not a good businessman, perhaps: too generous to be a good businessman; but as conscientious as the very devil, and with so fine a mathematical brain that he got over the practical difficulties.

'Tony was Senior Wrangler at Cambridge, and intended to go on with his mathematics. But then his uncle died, so he had to take over the business. You know what the business was then: three luxury hotels, built, equipped and run by Old Jim, the uncle, in Old Jim's most flamboyant style: all going to rack and ruin.

'Everybody said it was madness for Tony to push his shoulder up against the business world. His brother – that's

Stephen Marvell, the former surgeon – said Tony would only bring Old Jim's card houses down on everybody and swamp them all with more debts. But you know what happened. At twenty-five, Tony took over the business. At twenty-seven, he had the hotels on a paying basis. At thirty, they were hotels to which everybody went as a matter of course: blazing their sky signs, humming with efficiency, piling up profits which startled even Tony.

'And all because he sneered at the idea that there could be any such thing as overwork. He never let up. You can imagine that dogged expression of his: "Well, I don't like this work, but let's clean it up satisfactorily so that we can get on to more important things" – like his studies. He did it partly because he had promised Old Jim he would, and partly *because* (you see?) he thought the business so unimportant that he wanted to show how easy it was. But it wasn't easy. No man could stand that pace. London, Brighton, Eastbourne; he knew everything there was to know about the Marvell Hotels, down to the price of a pillowcase and the cost of grease for the lifts. At the end of the fifth year he collapsed one morning in his office. His brother Stephen told him what he had to do.

'"You're getting out of this," Stephen said. "You're going clear away. Round the world, anywhere; but for six or eight months at the shortest time. During that time, you're not even so much as to think of your work. Is that clear?"

'Tony told me the story himself last night. He says that the whole thing might never have happened if he had not been forbidden to write to anybody while he was away.

'"Not even so much as a postcard," snapped Stephen, "to

anybody. If you do, it'll be more business; and then God help you."

'"But Judith—" Tony protested.

'"Particularly to Judith," said Stephen. "If you insist on marrying your secretary, that's your affair. But you don't ruin your rest cure by exchanging long letters about the hotels."

'You can imagine Stephen's over-aristocratic, thin-nosed face towering over him, dull with anger. You can imagine Stephen in his black coat and striped trousers, standing up beside the polished desk of his office in Harley Street. Stephen Marvell (and, to a certain extent, Tony, too) had that over-bred air which Old Jim Marvell had always wanted and never achieved.

'Tony did not argue. He was willing enough, because he was tired. Even if he were forbidden to write to Judith, he could always think about her. In the middle of September, more than eight months ago, he sailed by the *Queen Anne* from Southampton. And on that night the terrors began.'

Hargreaves paused. The gas fire still hissed in the little, dim study. You would have known that this was a house in which death had occurred, and occurred recently, by the look on the face of Hargreaves' companion. He went on:

'The *Queen Anne* sailed at midnight. Tony saw her soaring up above the docks, as high as the sky. He saw the long decks, white and shiny like shoe boxes, gleaming under skeins of lights; he saw the black dots of passengers moving along them; he heard the click-rattle-rush of winches as great cranes swung over the crowd on the docks; and he felt the queer, pleasurable, restless feeling which stirs the nerves at the beginning of an ocean voyage.

24

'At first he was as excited as a schoolboy. Stephen Marvell and Judith Gates, Tony's fiancée, went down to Southampton with him. Afterwards he recalled talking to Judith; holding her arm, piloting her through the rubbery-smelling passages of the ship to show her how fine it was. They went to Tony's cabin, where his luggage had been piled together with a basket of fruit. Everybody agreed that it was a fine cabin.

'It was not until a few minutes before the "all-ashore" gong that the first pang of loneliness struck him. Stephen and Judith had already gone ashore, for all of them disliked these awkward, last-minute leave-takings. They were standing on the dock, far below. By leaning over the rail of the ship he could just see them. Judith's face was tiny, remote and smiling; infinitely loved. She was waving to him. Round him surged the crowd; faces, hats, noise under naked lights, accentuating the break with home, and water that would widen between. Next he heard the gong begin to bang: hollow, quivering, pulsing to loudness over the cry: "All ashore that's going ashore!"; and dying away into the ship. He did not want to go. There was still plenty of time. He could still gather up his luggage and get off.

'For a time he stood by the rail, with the breeze from Southampton Water in his face. Such a notion was foolish. He would stay. With a last wave to Judith and Stephen, he drew himself determinedly away. He would be sensible. He would go below and unpack his things. Feeling the unreality of that hollow night, he went down to his cabin on C Deck. And his luggage was not there! He stared round the stuffy cabin with its neat curtains at the portholes. There had been a trunk and two suitcases, gaudily labelled, to say nothing of the basket of fruit. Now the cabin was empty.

'Tony ran upstairs again to the purser's office. The purser, a harassed man behind a kind of ticket-window desk, was just getting rid of a clamouring crowd. In the intervals of striking a handbell and calling orders, he caught Tony's eye.

'"My luggage—" Tony said.

'"That's all right, Mr Marvell," said the harassed official. 'It's being taken ashore. But you'd better hurry yourself."

'Tony had here only a feeling of extreme stupidity. "Taken ashore?" he said. "But why? Who told you to send it ashore?"

'"Why, *you* did," said the purser, looking up suddenly from a sheet of names and figures.

'Tony only looked at him.

'"You came here," the purser went on, with sharply narrowing eyes, "not ten minutes ago. You said you had decided not to take the trip, and asked for your luggage to be taken off. I told you that at this late date we could not, of course, refund the—"

'"Get it back!" said Tony. His own voice sounded wrong. "I couldn't have told you that. Get it back!"

'"Just as you like, sir," said the purser, smiting on the bell, "*if* there's time."

'Overhead the hoarse blast of the whistle, that mournfullest of all sounds at sea, beat out against Southampton Water. B Deck, between open doors, was cold and gusty.

'Now, Tony Marvell had not the slightest recollection of having spoken to the purser before. That was what struck him between the eyes like a blow, and what, for the moment, almost drove him to run away from the *Queen Anne* before they should lift the gangplank. It was the nightmare again. One of the worst features of his nervous breakdown had been the conviction, coming in flashes at night, that he was not real any longer; that his body and his inner self had moved apart, the first walking or talking in everyday life like an articulate dummy, while the brain remained in another place. It was as though he were dead, and seeing his body move. Dead.

'To steady his wits, he tried to concentrate on familiar human things. Judith, for instance; he recalled Judith's hazel eyes, the soft line of her cheek as she turned her head, the paper cuffs she wore at the office. Judith, his fiancée, his secretary, who would take care of things while he was away; whom he loved, and who was so maddeningly close even now. But he must not think of Judith. Instead, he pictured his brother Stephen, and Johnny Cleaver, and any other friends who occurred to him. He even thought of Old Jim Marvell, who was dead. And – so strong is the power of imaginative visualisation – at that moment, in the breezy lounge room facing the purser's office, he thought he saw Old Jim looking at him round the corner of a potted palm.

'All this, you understand, went through Tony's mind in the brief second while he heard the ship's whistle hoot out over his head.

'He made some excuse to the purser, and went below. He was grateful for the chatter of noise, for the people passing up and down below decks. None of them paid any attention to him, but at least they were there. But, when he opened the door of his cabin, he stopped and stood very still in the doorway.

'The propellers had begun to churn. A throb, a heavy vibration, shook upwards through the ship; it made the tooth-glass tinkle in the rack, and sent a series of creaks through the bulkheads. The *Queen Anne* was moving. Tony Marvell took hold of the door as though that movement had been a lurch, and he stared at the bed across the cabin. On the white bedspread, where it had not been before, lay an automatic pistol.'

The gas fire had heated its asbestos pillars to glowing red. Again there was a brief silence in the little study of the house in St John's Wood. Hargreaves – Sir Charles Hargreaves, Assistant Commissioner of Police for the Criminal Investigation Department – leaned down and lowered the flame of the heater. Even the tone of his voice seemed to change when the gas ceased its loud hissing.

'Wait!' he said, lifting his hand. 'I don't want you to get the wrong impression. Don't think that the fear, the slow approach of what was going to happen, pursued Tony all through his trip round the world. It didn't. That's the most curious part of the whole affair.

'Tony has told me that it was a brief, bad bout, lasting perhaps fifteen minutes in all, just before and just after the *Queen Anne* sailed. It was not alone the uncanny feeling that things had ceased to be real. It was a sensation of active malignancy – of hatred, of danger, of what you like – surrounding him and pressing on him. He could feel it like a weak current from a battery.

'But five minutes after the ship had headed out to open sea, every such notion fell away from him. It was as though he had emerged out of an evil fog. That hardly seems reasonable. Even supposing that there are evil emanations, or evil spirits, it is difficult to think that they are confined to one country; that their tentacles are broken by half a mile's distance; that they cannot cross water. Yet there it was. One moment he was standing there with the automatic pistol in his hand, the noise of the engines beating in his ears and a horrible impulse joggling his elbow to put the muzzle of the pistol into his mouth and—

'Then – snap! Something broke: that is the only way he can describe it. He stood upright. He felt like a man coming out of a fever, shaken and sweating, but back from behind the curtain into the real world again. He gulped deep breaths. He went to the porthole and opened it. From that time on, he says, he began to get well.

'How the automatic had got into his cabin he did not know. He knew he must have brought it himself, in one of those blind flashes. But he could not remember. He stared at it with new eyes, and a new feeling of the beauty and sweetness of life. He felt as though he had been reprieved from execution.

'You might have thought that he would have flung the pistol overboard in sheer fear of touching it. But he didn't. To him it was the part of a puzzle. He stared much at it: a Browning .38, of Belgian manufacture, fully loaded. After the first few days, when he did keep it locked away out of sight in his trunk, he pondered over it. It represented the one piece of evidence he could carry back home with him, the one tangible reality in a nightmare.

'At the New York Customs shed it seemed to excite no

surprise. He carried it overland with him – Cleveland, Chicago, Salt Lake City – to San Francisco, in a fog, and then down the kindled sea to Honolulu. At Yokohama they were going to take it away from him; only a huge bribe retrieved it. Afterwards he carried it on his person, and was never searched. As the broken bones of his nerves knitted, as in the wash of the propellers, there was peace, it became a kind of mascot. It went with him through the blistering heat of the Indian Ocean, into the murky Red Sea, to the Mediterranean. To Port Said, to Cairo in early winter. To Naples and Marseilles and Gibraltar. It was tucked away in his hip-pocket on the bitter cold night, a little more than eight months after his departure, when Tony Marvell – a healed man again – landed back at Southampton in the SS *Chippenham Castle*.

'It was snowing that night, you remember? The boat train roared through thickening snow. It was crowded, and the heat would not work.

'Tony knew that there could be nobody at Southampton to meet him. His itinerary had been laid out in advance, and he had stuck to the bitter letter of his instructions about not writing even so much as a postcard. But he had altered the itinerary, so as to take a ship that would get him home in time for Christmas; he would burst in on them a week early. For eight months he had lived in a void. In an hour or two he would be home. He would see Judith again.

'In the dimly lighted compartment of the train, his fellow passengers were not talkative. The long voyage had squeezed their conversation dry; they almost hated each other. Even the snow roused only a flicker of enthusiasm.

'"Real old-fashioned Christmas!" said one.

'"Hah!" said another appreciatively, scratching with his fingernails at the frosted window.

'"Damn cold, *I* call it," snarled a third. "Can't they ever make the heat work in these trains? I'm damn well going to make a complaint!"

'After that, with a sympathetic grunt or mutter, each retired behind his newspaper; a white, blank wall which rustled occasionally, and behind which they drank up news of home.

'In other words (Tony remembers that he thought then), he was in England again. He was home. For himself, he only pretended to read. He leaned back in his seat, listening vaguely to the clackety-roar of the wheels, and the long blast of the whistle that was torn behind as the train gathered speed.

'He knew exactly what he would do. It would be barely ten o'clock when they reached Waterloo. He would jump into a cab, and hurry home – to this house – for a wash and brush-up. Then he would pelt up to Judith's flat at Hampstead as hard as he could go. Yet this thought, which should have made him glow, left him curiously chilly round the heart. He fought the chill. He laughed at himself. Determinedly he opened the newspaper, distracting himself, turning from page to page, running his eye down each column. Then he stopped. Something familiar caught his eye, some familiar name. It was an obscure item on a middle page.

'He was reading in this paper the news of his own death. Just that.

Mr Anthony Dean Marvell, of Upper Avenue Road, St John's Wood, and owner of Marvell Hotels, Ltd, was found shot dead last night in his bedroom at home. A bullet had penetrated up through the roof of the mouth into the brain, and a small-calibre automatic was in his hand. The body was found by Mrs Reach, Mr Marvell's housekeeper, who ...

'A suicide!

'And once again, as suddenly as it had left him aboard ship, the grasp fell on him, shutting him off from the real world into the unreal. The compartment, as I told you, was very dimly lighted. So it was perhaps natural that he could only dimly see a blank wall of upheld newspapers facing him; as though there were no fellow passengers there, as though they had deserted him in a body, leaving only the screen of papers that joggled a little with the rush of the train.

'Yes, he was alone.

'He got up blindly, dragging open the door of the compartment to get out into the corridor. The confined space seemed to be choking him. Holding his own newspaper up high, so as to catch the light from the compartment, he read the item again.

'There could be no possibility of a mistake. The account was too detailed. It told all about him, his past and present ...

... His brother, Mr Stephen Marvell, the eminent Harley Street surgeon, was hurriedly summoned ... His fiancée, Miss Judith Gates ... It is understood that in September Mr Marvell suffered a nervous breakdown, from which even a long rest had not effected a cure ...

'Tony looked at the date of the newspaper, afraid of what he might see. But it was the date of that day: the twenty-third of December. From this account, it appeared that he had shot himself forty-eight hours before.

'And the gun was in his hip-pocket now.

'Tony folded up the newspaper. The train moved under his feet with a dancing sway, jerking above the click of the wheels; and another thin blast of the whistle went by. It reminded him of the whistle aboard the *Queen Anne*. He glanced along the dusky corridor. It was empty except for someone, whom he supposed to be another passenger, leaning elbows on the rail past the windows and staring out at the flying snow.

'He remembers nothing else until the train reached Waterloo. But something – an impression, a subconscious memory – registered in his mind about that passenger he had seen in the corridor. First it had to do with the shape of the person's shoulders. Then Tony realised that this was because the person was wearing a greatcoat with an old-fashioned brown fur collar. He was jumping blindly out of the train at Waterloo when he remembered that Old Jim Marvell always used to wear such a collar.

'After that he seemed to see it everywhere.

'When he hurried up to the guard's van to claim his trunk and suitcases, the luggage ticket in his hand, he was in such a crowd that he could not move his arms. But he thought he felt brown fur press the back of his shoulders.

'A porter got him a taxi. It was a relief to see a London cab again, in a coughing London terminus, and hear the bump of the trunk as it went up under the strap, and friendly voices again. He gave the address to the driver, tipped the porter, and jumped inside. Even so, the porter seemed to be holding open the door of the taxi longer than was necessary.

'"Close it, man!" Tony found himself shouting. "Close it, quick!"

'"Yessir," said the porter, jumping back. The door slammed. Afterwards, the porter stood and stared after the taxi. Tony, glancing out through the little back window, saw him still standing there.

'It was dark in the cab, and as close as though a photographer's black hood had been drawn over him. Tony could see little. But he carefully felt with his hands all over the seat, all over the open space; and he found nothing.'

At this point in the story, Hargreaves broke off for a moment or two. He had been speaking with difficulty; not as though he expected to be doubted, but as though the right words were hard to find. His gloved fingers opened and closed on his knee.

For the first time his companion – Miss Judith Gates – interrupted him. Judith spoke from the shadow on the other side of the gas fire.

'Wait!' she said. 'Please!'

'Yes?' said Hargreaves.

'This person who was following Tony.' She spoke also with difficulty. 'You aren't telling me that it was – well, was—?'

'Was what?'

'Dead,' said Judith.

'I don't know who it was,' answered Hargreaves, looking at her steadily. 'Except that it seemed to be somebody with a fur collar on his coat. I'm telling you Tony's story, which I believe.'

Judith's hand shaded her eyes. 'All the same,' she insisted, and her pleasant voice went high, 'even supposing it was! I mean, even supposing it was the person you think. *He* of all people, living or dead, wouldn't have tried to put any evil influence round Tony. Old Jim loved Tony. He left Tony every penny he owned, and not a farthing to Stephen. He always told Tony he'd look after him.'

'And so he did,' said Hargreaves.

'But—'

'You see,' Hargreaves told her slowly. 'You still don't understand the source of the evil influence. Tony didn't, himself. All he knew was that he was bowling along in a dark taxi, through slippery, snowy streets; and whatever might be following him, good or bad, he couldn't endure it.

'Even so, everything might have ended well if the taxi driver had been careful. But he wasn't. That was the first snowfall of the year, and the driver miscalculated. When they were only two hundred yards from Upper Avenue Road, he tried to take a turn too fast. Tony felt the helpless swing of the skid; he saw the glass partition tilt, and a black tree trunk rush up, huge, at them until it exploded against the outer windscreen. They landed upright against the tree, with a buckled wheel.

'"I *'ad* to swerve," the driver was crying. "I *'ad* to! An old gent with a fur collar walked smack out in front of—"

'And so, you see, Tony had to walk home alone.

'He knew something was following him before he had taken

half a dozen steps. Two hundred yards doesn't sound like a great distance. First right, first left, and you're home. But here it seemed to stretch out interminably, as such things do in dreams. He did not want to leave the taxi driver. The driver thought this was because Tony doubted his honesty about bringing the luggage on when the wheel was repaired. But it was not that.

'For the first part of the way, Tony walked rapidly. The other thing walked at an equal pace behind him. By the light of a street lamp Tony could see the wet fur collar on the coat, but nothing else. Afterwards he increased his pace to what was almost a run; and, though no difference could be seen in the gait of what was behind him, it was still there. Unlike you, Tony didn't wonder whether it might be good or evil. These nice differences don't occur to you when you're dealing with something that may be dead. All he knew was that he mustn't let it *identify* itself with him or he was done for.

'Then it began to gain on him, and he ran.

'The pavement was black, the snow dirty grey. He saw the familiar turning, where front gardens were built up above the low stone walls; he saw the street sign fastened to one of those corners, white lettering on black; and, in sudden blind panic, he plunged for the steps that led up to his home.

'The house was dark. He got the cold keys out of his pocket, but the keyring slipped round in his fingers, like soap in bath water, and fell on the tiled floor of the vestibule. He groped after it in the dark – just as the thing turned in at the gate. In fact, Tony heard the gate creak. He found the keys, found the lock by a miracle, and opened the door.

'But he was too late, because the other thing was already coming up the front steps. Tony says that at close range, against a street lamp, the fur collar looked more wet and moth-eaten; that is all he can describe. He was in a dark hall with the door open. Even familiar things had fled his wits and he could not remember the position of the light switch.

'The other person walked in.

'In his hip-pocket, Tony remembered, he still had the weapon he had carried round the world. He fumbled under his overcoat to get the gun out of his pocket; but even that weak gesture was no good for him, for he dropped the gun on the carpet. Since the visitor was now within six feet of him, he did not stop. He bolted up the stairs.

'At the top of the stairs he risked a short glance down. The other thing had stopped. In faint bluish patches of light which came through the open front door, Tony could see that it was stooping down to pick up the automatic pistol from the carpet.

'Tony thinks – now – that he began to switch on lights in the upper hall. Also, he shouted something. He was standing before the door of his bedroom. He threw open this door, blundered in, and began to turn on more lamps. He had got two lamps lighted before he turned to look at the bed, which was occupied.

'The man on the bed did not, however, sit up at the coming of noise or lights. A sheet covered him from head to feet; and even under the outline of the sheet you could trace the line of the wasted, sunken features. Tony Marvell then did what was perhaps the most courageous act of his life. He had to know. He walked across and turned down the upper edge of the sheet, and looked down at his own face; a dead face, turned sightlessly up from the bed.

'Shock? Yes. But more terror? No. For this dead man was real, he was flesh and blood – as Tony was flesh and blood. He looked exactly like Tony. But it was now no question of a real world and an unreal world; it was no question of going mad. This man was real; and that meant fraud and imposture.

'A voice from across the room said: "*So you're alive*!" And Tony turned round, to find his brother Stephen looking at him from the doorway.

'Stephen wore a red dressing gown, hastily pulled round him, and his hair was tousled. His face was one of collapse.

'"I didn't mean to do it!" Stephen was crying out at him. Even though Tony did not understand, he felt that the words were a confession of guilt; they were babbling words, words which made you pity the man who said them.

'"I never really meant to have you killed aboard that ship," said Stephen. "It was all a joke. You know I wouldn't have hurt you; you know that, don't you? Listen—"

'Now Stephen (as I said) was standing in the doorway, clutching his dressing gown round him. What made him look round towards the hall behind, quickly, Tony did not know. Perhaps he heard a sound behind him. Perhaps he saw something out of the corner of his eye. But Stephen did look round, and he began to scream.

'Tony saw no more, for the light in the hall went out. The fear was back on him again, and he could not move. For he saw a hand. It was only, so to speak, the flicker of a hand. This hand darted in from the darkness out in the hall; it caught hold of the knob on the bedroom door, and closed the door. It turned a key on the outside, locking Tony into the room. It kept Stephen outside in the dark hall – and Stephen was still screaming.

'A good thing, too, that Tony had been locked in the room. That saved trouble with the police afterwards.

'The rest of the testimony comes from Mrs Reach, the housekeeper. Her room was next door to Stephen's bedroom, at the end of the upstairs hall. She was awakened by screams, by what seemed to be thrashing sounds, and the noise of hard breathing. These sounds passed her door towards Stephen's room.

'Just as she was getting out of her bed and putting on a dressing gown, she heard Stephen's door close. Just as she went out into the hall, she heard, for the second time in forty-eight hours, the noise of a pistol shot.

'Now, Mrs Reach will testify in a coroner's court that nobody left, or could have left Stephen's room after the shot. She was looking at the door, though it was several minutes before she could screw up enough courage to open the door. When she did open it, all sounds had ceased. He had been shot through the right temple at close range; presumably by himself, since the weapon was discovered in a tangle of stained bed clothing. There was nobody else in the room, and all the windows were locked on the inside. The only other thing Mrs Reach noticed was an unpleasant – an intensely unpleasant – smell of mildewed cloth and wet fur.'

Again Hargreaves paused. It seemed that he had come to the end of the story. An outsider might have thought, too, that he had emphasised these horrors too much, for the girl across from him kept her hands pressed against her eyes. But Hargreaves knew his business.

'Well?' he said gently. 'You see the explanation, don't you?'

Judith took her hands away from her eyes. 'Explanation?'

'The natural explanation,' repeated Hargreaves, spacing his words. 'Tony Marvell is not going mad. He never had any brainstorms or "blind flashes". He only thought he had. The whole thing was a cruel and murderous fake, engineered by Stephen, and it went wrong. But if it had succeeded, Stephen Marvell would have committed a very nearly perfect murder.'

The relief he saw flash across Judith's face, the sudden dazed catching at hope, went to Hargreaves' heart. But he did not show this.

'Let's go back eight months,' he went on, 'and take it from the beginning. Now, Tony is a very wealthy young man. The distinguished Stephen, on the other hand, was swamped with debts and always on the thin edge of bankruptcy. If Tony were to die, Stephen, the next of kin, would inherit the whole estate. So Stephen decided that Tony had to die.

'But Stephen, a medical man, knew the risks of murder. No matter how cleverly you plan it, there is always *some* suspicion; and Stephen was bound to be suspected. He was unwilling to risk those prying detectives, those awkward questions, those damning postmortem reports – until, more than eight months ago, he suddenly saw how he could destroy Tony without the smallest suspicion attaching to himself.

'In St Jude's Hospital, where he did some charity work, Stephen had found a broken-down ex-schoolmaster named

Rupert Hayes. Every man in this world, they say, has his exact double. Hayes was Tony's double to the slightest feature. He was, in fact, so uncannily like Tony that the very sight of him made Stephen flinch. Now, Hayes was dying of tuberculosis. He had, at most, not more than a year to live. He would be eager to listen to any scheme which would allow him to spend the rest of his life in luxury, and die of natural causes in a soft bed. To him Stephen explained the trick.

'Tony should be ordered off – apparently – on a trip round the world. On the night he was to sail, Tony should be allowed to go aboard.

'Hayes should be waiting aboard that same ship, with a gun in his pocket. After Stephen or any other friends had left the ship conveniently early, Hayes should entice Tony up to the dark boat deck. Then he was to shoot Tony through the head, and drop the body overboard.

'Haven't you ever realised that a giant ocean liner, just before it leaves port, is the ideal place to commit a murder? Not a soul will remember you afterwards. The passengers notice nothing; they are too excited. The crew notice nothing; they are kept too busy. The confusion of the crowd is intense. And what happens to your victim after he goes overboard? He will be sucked under and presently caught by the terrible propellers, to make him unrecognisable. When a body is found – if it is found at all – it will be presumed to be some dock-roysterer. Certainly it will never be connected with the ocean liner, because there will be nobody missing from the liner's passenger list.

'Missing from the passenger list? Of course not! Hayes,

you see, was to go to the purser and order Tony's luggage to be sent ashore. He was to say he was cancelling the trip, and not going after all. After killing Tony he was then to walk ashore as—'

The girl uttered an exclamation.

Hargreaves nodded. 'You see it now. He was to walk ashore *as Tony*. He was to say to his friends that he couldn't face the journey after all; and everybody would be happy. Why not? The real Tony was within an ace of doing just that.

'Then, Hayes, well coached, would simply settle down to play the part of Tony for the rest of his natural life. Mark that: his natural life; a year at most. He would be too ill to attend to the business, of course. He wouldn't even see you, his fiancée, too often. If ever he made any bad slips, that, of course, would be his bad nerves. He would be allowed to "develop" lung trouble. At the end of a year, amid sorrowing friends …

'Stephen had planned brilliantly. "Murder"? What do you mean, murder? Let the doctors examine as much as they like! Let the police ask what questions they like! Whatever steps are taken, Stephen Marvell is absolutely safe. For the poor devil in bed really has died a natural death.

'Only – well, it went wrong. Hayes wasn't cut out to be a murderer. I hadn't the favour of his acquaintance, but he must have been a decent sort. He promised to do this. But, when it came to the actual fact, he couldn't force himself to kill Tony: literally, physically couldn't. He threw away his pistol and ran. On the other hand, once off the ship, he couldn't confess to Stephen that Tony was still alive. He couldn't give up that year of sweet luxury, with all Tony's money at his disposal to soothe his aching lungs. So he pretended to Stephen that he had done the job, and Stephen danced for joy. But Hayes, as the months went on, did not dance. He knew Tony wasn't dead. He knew there would be a reckoning soon. And he couldn't let it end like that. A week before he thought Tony was coming home, after writing a letter to the police to explain everything, Hayes shot himself rather than face exposure.'

There was a silence. 'That, I think,' Hargreaves said quietly, 'explains everything about Tony.'

Judith Gates bit her lips. Her pretty face was working; and she could not control the twitching of her capable hands. For a moment she seemed to be praying.

'Thank God!' she murmured. 'I was afraid—'

'Yes,' said Hargreaves; 'I know.'

'But it still doesn't explain everything. It—'

Hargreaves stopped her.

'I said,' he pointed out, 'that it explains everything about Tony. That's all you need worry about. Tony is free. You are free. As for Stephen Marvell's death, it was suicide. That is the official record.'

'But that's absurd!' cried Judith. 'I didn't like Stephen; I always knew he hated Tony; but he wasn't one to kill himself, even if he were exposed. Don't you see, you haven't explained the one real horror? I must know. I mean, I must know if you think what I think about it. Who was the man with the brown fur collar? Who followed Tony home that night? Who stuck close by him, to keep the evil influences off him? Who was his guardian? Who shot Stephen in revenge?'

Sir Charles Hargreaves looked down at the sputtering gas fire. His face, inscrutable, was wrinkled in sharp lines from mouth to nostril. His brain held many secrets. He was ready to lock away this one, once he knew that they understood each other.

'You tell me,' he said.

A Very Commonplace Murder

P.D. James

'We close at twelve on Saturday,' said the blonde in the estate office. 'So if you keep the key after then, please drop it back through the letter box. It's the only key we have, and there may be other people wanting to view on Monday. Sign here, please, sir.'

The 'sir' was grudging, an afterthought. Her tone was reproving. She didn't really think he would buy the flat, this seedy old man with his air of spurious gentility, with his harsh voice. In her job you soon got a nose for the genuine enquirer. Ernest Gabriel. An odd name, half-common, half-fancy.

But he took the key politely enough and thanked her for her trouble. No trouble, she thought. God knew there were few enough people interested in that sordid little dump, not at the price they were asking. He could keep the key a week, for all she cared.

She was right. Gabriel hadn't come to buy, only to view. It was the first time he had been back since it all happened sixteen years ago. He came neither as a pilgrim nor a penitent. He had returned under some compulsion which he hadn't even bothered to analyse. He had been on his way to visit his only living relative, an elderly aunt, who had recently been admitted to a geriatric ward. He hadn't even realised the bus would pass the flat.

But suddenly they were lurching through Camden Town, and the road became familiar, like a photograph springing into focus; and with a frisson of surprise he recognised the double-fronted shop and the flat above. There was an estate agent's notice in the window. Almost without thinking, he had got off at the next stop, gone back to verify the name, and walked the half-mile to the office. It had seemed as natural and inevitable as his daily bus journey to work.

Twenty minutes later he fitted the key into the lock of the front door and passed into the stuffy emptiness of the flat. The grimy walls still held the smell of cooking. There was a spatter of envelopes on the worn linoleum, dirtied and trampled by the feet of previous viewers. The light bulb swung naked in the hall, and the door into the sitting room stood open. To his right was the staircase, to his left the kitchen.

Gabriel paused for a moment, then went into the kitchen. From the windows, half-curtained with grubby gingham, he looked upward to the great black building at the rear of the flat, eyeless except for the one small square of window high on the fifth floor. It was from this window, sixteen years ago,

46

that he had watched Denis Speller and Eileen Morrisey play out their commonplace little tragedy to its end.

He had no right to be watching them, no right to be in the building at all after six o'clock. That had been the nub of his awful dilemma. It had happened by chance. Mr Maurice Bootman had instructed him, as the firm's filing clerk, to go through the papers in the late Mr Bootman's upstairs den in case there were any which should be in the files. They weren't confidential or important papers – those had been dealt with by the family and the firm's solicitors months before. They were just a miscellaneous, yellowing collection of out-of-date memoranda, old accounts, receipts, and fading press clippings which had been bundled together into old Mr Bootman's desk. He had been a great hoarder of trivia.

But at the back of the left-hand bottom drawer Gabriel had found a key. It was by chance that he tried it in the lock of the corner cupboard. It fitted. And in the cupboard Gabriel found the late Mr Bootman's small but choice collection of pornography.

He knew that he had to read the books; not just to snatch surreptitious minutes with one ear listening for a footstep on the stairs or the whine of the approaching elevator, and fearful always that his absence from his filing room would be noticed. No, he had to read them in privacy and in peace. So he devised his plan.

It wasn't difficult. As a trusted member of the staff, he had one of the Yale keys to the side door at which goods were delivered. It was locked on the inside at night by the porter before he went off duty. It wasn't difficult for Gabriel, always among the last to leave, to find the opportunity of shooting back the bolts before leaving with the porter by the main door. He dared risk it only once a week, and the day he chose was Friday.

He would hurry home, eat his solitary meal beside the gas fire in his bed-sitting room, then make his way back to the building and let himself in by the side door. All that was necessary was to make sure he was waiting for the office to open on Monday morning so that, among the first in, he could lock the side door before the porter made his ritual visit to unlock it for the day's deliveries.

These Friday nights became a desperate but shameful joy to Gabriel. Their pattern was always the same. He would sit crouched in old Mr Bootman's low leather chair in front of the fireplace, his shoulders hunched over the book in his lap, his eyes following the pool of light from his torch as it moved over each page. He never dared to switch on the room light, and even on the coldest night he never lit the gas fire. He was fearful that its hiss might mask the sound of approaching feet, that its glow might shine through the thick curtains at the window, or that, somehow, the smell of gas would linger in the room next Monday morning to betray him. He was morbidly afraid of discovery, yet even this fear added to the excitement of his secret pleasure.

It was on the third Friday in January that he first saw them. It was a mild evening, but heavy and starless. An early rain had slimed the pavements and bled the scribbled headlines from the newspaper placards. Gabriel wiped his feet carefully before climbing to the fifth floor. The claustrophobic room smelled sour and dusty, the air struck colder than the night outside. He wondered whether he dared open the window and let in some of the sweetness of the rain-cleansed sky.

It was then that he saw the woman. Below him were the back entrances of the two shops, each with a flat above. One flat had boarded windows, but the other looked lived in. It was approached by a flight of iron steps leading to an asphalt yard. He saw the woman in the glow of a street lamp as she paused at the foot of the steps, fumbling in her handbag. Then, as if gaining resolution, she came swiftly up the steps and almost ran across the asphalt to the flat door.

He watched as she pressed herself into the shadow of the doorway, then swiftly turned the key in the lock and slid out of his sight. He had time only to notice that she was wearing a pale mackintosh buttoned high under a mane of fairish hair and that she carried a string bag of what looked like groceries. It seemed an oddly furtive and solitary homecoming.

Gabriel waited. Almost immediately he saw the light go on in the room to the left of the door. Perhaps she was in the kitchen. He could see her faint shadow passing to and fro, bending and then lengthening. He guessed that she was unpacking the groceries. Then the light in the room went out.

For a few moments the flat was in darkness. Then the light in the upstairs window went on, brighter this time, so that he could see the woman more plainly. She could not know how plainly. The curtains were drawn, but they were thin. Perhaps the owners, confident that they were not overlooked, had grown careless. Although the woman's silhouette was only a faint blur, Gabriel could see that she was carrying a tray. Perhaps she was intending to eat her supper in bed. She was undressing now.

He could see her lifting the garments over her head and twisting down to release stockings and take off her shoes. Suddenly she came very close to the window, and he saw the outline of her body plainly. She seemed to be watching and listening. Gabriel found that he was holding his breath. Then she moved away, and the light dimmed. He guessed that she had switched off the central bulb and was using the bedside lamp. The room was now lit with a softer, pinkish glow within which the woman moved, insubstantial as a dream.

Gabriel stood with his face pressed against the cold window, still watching. Shortly after eight o'clock the boy arrived. Gabriel always thought of him as 'the boy'. Even from that distance his youth, his vulnerability, were apparent. He approached the flat with more confidence than the woman, but still swiftly, pausing at the top of the steps as if to assess the width of the rain-washed yard.

She must have been waiting for his knock. She let him in at once, the door barely opening. Gabriel knew that she had come naked to let him in. And then there were two shadows in the upstairs room, shadows that met and parted and came together again before they moved, joined, to the bed and out of Gabriel's sight.

The next Friday he watched to see if they would come again. They did, and at the same times, the woman first, at twenty minutes past seven, the boy forty minutes later. Again Gabriel stood, rigidly intent at his watching post, as the light in the upstairs window sprang on and then was lowered. The two naked figures, seen dimly behind the curtains, moved to and fro, joined and parted, fused and swayed together in a ritualistic parody of a dance.

This Friday Gabriel waited until they left. The boy came out first, sidling quickly from the half-open door and almost leaping down the steps, as if in exultant joy. The woman followed five minutes later, locking the door behind her and darting across the asphalt, her head bent.

After that he watched for them every Friday. They held a fascination for him even greater than Mr Bootman's books. Their routine hardly varied. Sometimes the boy arrived a little late, and Gabriel would see the woman watching motionless for him behind the bedroom curtains. He too would stand with held breath, sharing her agony of impatience, willing the boy to come. Usually the boy carried a bottle under his arm, but one week it was in a wine basket, and he bore it with great care. Perhaps it was an anniversary, a special evening for them. Always the woman had the bag of groceries. Always they ate together in the bedroom.

Friday after Friday Gabriel stood in the darkness, his eyes fixed on that upstairs window, straining to decipher the outlines of their naked bodies, picturing what they were doing to each other.

They had been meeting for seven weeks when it happened. Gabriel was late at the building that night. His usual bus did not run, and the first to arrive was full. By the time he reached his watching post, there was already a light in the bedroom. He pressed his face to the window, his hot breath smearing the pane. Hastily rubbing it clear with the cuff of his coat, he looked again. For a moment he thought that there were two figures in the bedroom. But that must surely be a freak of the light. The boy wasn't due for thirty minutes yet. But the woman, as always, was on time.

Twenty minutes later he went into the washroom on the floor below. He had become much more confident during the last few weeks and now moved about the building, silently, and using only his torch for light, but with almost as much assurance as during the day. He spent nearly ten minutes in the washroom. His watch showed that it was just after eight by the time he was back at the window, and, at first, he thought that he had missed the boy. But no, the slight figure was even now running up the steps and across the asphalt to the shelter of the doorway.

Gabriel watched as he knocked and waited for the door to open. But it didn't open. She didn't come. There was a light in the bedroom, but no shadow moved on the curtains. The boy knocked again. Gabriel could just detect the quivering of his knuckles against the door. Again he waited. Then the boy drew back and looked up at the lighted window. Perhaps he was risking a low-pitched call. Gabriel could hear nothing, but he could sense the tension in that waiting figure.

Again the boy knocked. Again there was no response. Gabriel watched and suffered with him until, at twenty past eight, the boy finally gave up and turned away. Then Gabriel too stretched his cramped limbs and made his way into the night. The wind was rising and a young moon reeled through the torn clouds. It was getting colder. He wore no coat and missed its comfort. Hunching his shoulders against the bite of the wind, he knew that this was the last Friday he would come late to the building. For him, as for that desolate boy, it was the end of a chapter.

He first read about the murder in his morning paper on his way to work the following Monday. He recognised the picture of the flat at once, although it looked oddly unfamiliar with the bunch of plainclothes detectives conferring at the door and the stolid uniformed policeman at the top of the steps.

The story so far was slight. A Mrs Eileen Morrisey, aged thirty-four, had been found stabbed to death in a flat in Camden Town late on Sunday night. The discovery was made by the tenants, Mr and Mrs Kealy, who had returned late on Sunday from a visit to Mr Kealy's parents. The dead woman, who was the mother of twin daughters aged twelve, was a friend of Mrs Kealy. Detective Chief Inspector William Holbrook was in charge of the investigation. It was understood that the dead woman had been sexually assaulted.

Gabriel folded his paper with the same precise care as he did on any ordinary day. Of course, he would have to tell the police what he had seen. He couldn't let an innocent man suffer, no matter what the inconvenience to himself. The knowledge of his intention, of his public-spirited devotion to justice, was warmly satisfying. For the rest of the day he crept around his filing cabinets with the secret complacency of a man dedicated to sacrifice.

But somehow his first plan of calling at a police station on his way home from work came to nothing. There was no point in acting hastily. If the boy were arrested, he would speak. But it would be ridiculous to prejudice his reputation and endanger his job before he even knew whether the boy was a suspect. The police might never learn of the boy's existence. To speak up now might only focus suspicion on the innocent. A prudent man would wait. Gabriel decided to be prudent.

The boy was arrested three days later. Again Gabriel read about it in his morning paper. There was no picture this time, and few details. The news had to compete with a society elopement and a major air crash and did not make the first page. The inch of newsprint stared briefly: 'Denis John Speller, a butcher's assistant, aged nineteen, who gave an address at Muswell Hill, was today charged with the murder of Mrs Eileen Morrisey, the mother of twelve-year-old twins, who was stabbed to death last Friday in a flat in Camden Town.'

So the police now knew more precisely the time of death. Perhaps it was time for him to see them. But how could he be sure that this Denis Speller was the young lover he had been watching these past Friday nights? A woman like that – well, she might have had any number of men. No photograph of the accused would be published in any paper until after the trial. But more information would come out at the preliminary hearing. He would wait for that. After all, the accused might not even be committed for trial.

Besides, he had himself to consider. There had been time to think of his own position. If young Speller's life were in danger, then, of course, Gabriel would tell what he had seen. But it would mean the end of his job with Bootman's. Worse, he would never get another. Mr Maurice Bootman would see to that. He, Gabriel, would be branded as a dirty-minded, sneaking little voyeur, a Peeping Tom who was willing to jeopardise his livelihood for an hour or two with a naughty book and a chance to pry into other people's happiness. Mr Maurice would be too angry at the publicity to forgive the man who had caused it.

And the rest of the firm would laugh. It would be the best

joke in years, funny and pathetic and futile. The pedantic, respectable, censorious Ernest Gabriel found out at last! And they wouldn't even give him credit for speaking up. It simply wouldn't occur to them that he could have kept silent.

If only he could think of a good reason for being in the building that night. But there was none. He could hardly say that he had stayed behind to work late, when he had taken such care to leave with the porter. And it wouldn't do to say that he had returned later to catch up with his filing. His filing was always up-to-date, as he was fond of pointing out. His very efficiency was against him.

Besides, he was a poor liar. The police wouldn't accept his story without probing. After they had spent so much time on the case they would hardly welcome his tardy revelation of new evidence. He pictured the circle of grim, accusing faces, the official civility barely concealing their dislike and contempt. There was no sense in inviting such an ordeal before he was sure of the facts.

But after the preliminary hearing, at which Denis Speller was sent up for trial, the same arguments seemed equally valid. By now he knew that Speller was the lover he had seen. There had never really been much room for doubt. By now, too, the outlines of the case for the Crown were apparent. The prosecution would seek to prove that this was a crime of passion, that the boy, tormented by her threat to leave him, had killed in jealousy or revenge. The accused would deny that he had entered the flat that night, would state again and again that he had knocked and gone away. Only Gabriel could support his story. But it would still be premature to speak.

He decided to attend the trial. In that way he would hear the strength of the Crown's case. If it appeared likely that the verdict would be 'Not Guilty', he could remain silent. And if things went badly, there was an excitement, a fearful fascination, in the thought of rising to his feet in the silence of that crowded court and speaking out his evidence before all the world. The questioning, the criticism, the notoriety would come later. But he would have had his moment of glory.

He was surprised and a little disappointed by the court. He had expected a more imposing, more dramatic setting for justice than this modern, clean-smelling, businesslike room. Everything was quiet and orderly. There was no crowd at the door jostling for seats. It wasn't even a popular trial.

Sliding into his seat at the back of the court, Gabriel looked round, at first apprehensively and then with more confidence. But he needn't have worried. There was no one there he knew. It was really a very dull collection of people, hardly worthy, he thought, of the drama that was to be played out before them. Some of them looked as if they might have worked with Speller or lived in the same street. All looked ill-at-ease, with the slightly furtive air of people who find themselves in unusual or intimidating surroundings. There was a thin woman in black crying softly into a handkerchief. No one took any notice of her; no one comforted her.

From time to time one of the doors at the back of the court would open silently, and a newcomer would sidle almost furtively into his seat. When this happened, the row of faces would turn momentarily to him without interest, without recognition, before turning their eyes again to the slight figure in the dock.

Gabriel stared too. At first he dared to cast only fleeting glances, averting his eyes suddenly, as if each glance were a desperate risk. It was unthinkable that the prisoner's eyes should meet his, should somehow know that here was the man who could save him and should signal a desperate appeal. But when he had risked two or three glances, he realised that there was nothing to fear. That solitary figure was seeing no one, caring about no one except himself. He was only a bewildered and terrified boy, his eyes turned inward to some private hell. He looked like a trapped animal, beyond hope and beyond fight.

The judge was rotund, red-faced, his chins sunk into the bands at his neck. He had small hands, which he rested on the desk before him except when he was making notes. Then counsel would stop talking for a moment before continuing more slowly, as if anxious not to hurry his Lordship, watching him like a worried father explaining with slow deliberation to a not very bright child.

But Gabriel knew where lay the power. The judge's chubby hands, folded on the desk like a parody of a child in prayer, held a man's life in their grasp. There was only one person in the court with more power than that scarlet-sashed figure high under the carved coat-of-arms. And that was he, Gabriel. The realisation came to him in a spurt of exultation, at once intoxicating and satisfying. He hugged his knowledge to himself gloatingly. This was a new sensation, terrifyingly sweet.

He looked round at the solemn watching faces and wondered how they would change if he got suddenly to his feet and called out what he knew. He would say it firmly, confidently. They wouldn't be able to frighten him. He would say, 'My Lord. The accused is innocent. He did knock and go away. I, Gabriel, saw him.'

And then what would happen? It was impossible to guess. Would the judge stop the trial so that they could all adjourn to his chambers and hear his evidence in private? Or would Gabriel be called now to take his stand in the witness box? One thing was certain – there would be no fuss, no hysteria.

But suppose the judge merely ordered him out of the court. Suppose he was too surprised to take in what Gabriel had said. Gabriel could picture him leaning forward irritably, hand to his ear, while the police at the back of the court came silently forward to drag out the offender. Surely in this calm, aseptic atmosphere, where justice itself seemed an academic ritual, the voice of truth would be merely a vulgar intrusion. No one would believe him. No one would listen. They had set this elaborate scene to play out their drama to the end. They wouldn't thank him for spoiling it now. The time to speak had passed.

Even if they did believe him, he wouldn't get any credit now for coming forward. He would be blamed for leaving it so late, for letting an innocent man get so close to the gallows. If Speller were innocent, of course. And who could tell that? They would say that he might have knocked and gone away, only to return later and gain access to kill. He, Gabriel, hadn't waited at the window to see. So his sacrifice would have been for nothing.

And he could hear those taunting office voices: 'Trust old Gabriel to leave it to the last minute. Bloody coward. Read any naughty books lately, Archangel?' He would be sacked from Bootman's without even the consolation of standing well in the public eye.

Oh, he would make the headlines, all right. He could imagine them: 'Outburst in Old Bailey'. 'Man Upholds Accused's Alibi'. Only it wasn't an alibi. What did it really prove? He would be regarded as a public nuisance, the pathetic little voyeur who was too much of a coward to go to the police earlier. And Denis Speller would still hang.

Once the moment of temptation had passed and he knew with absolute certainty that he wasn't going to speak, Gabriel began almost to enjoy himself. After all, it wasn't every day that one could watch British justice at work. He listened, noted, appreciated. It was a formidable case which the prosecution unfolded. Gabriel approved of the prosecuting counsel. With his high forehead, beaked nose and bony, intelligent face, he looked so much more distinguished than the judge. This was how a famous lawyer should look. He made his case without passion, almost without interest. But that, Gabriel knew, was how the law worked. It wasn't the duty of prosecuting counsel to work for a conviction. His job was to state with fairness and accuracy the case for the Crown.

He called his witnesses. Mrs Brenda Kealy, the wife of the tenant of the flat. A blonde, smartly dressed, common little slut if ever Gabriel saw one. Oh, he knew her type, all right. He could guess what his mother would have said about her. Anyone could see what she was interested in. And by the look of her, she was getting it regularly, too. Dressed up for a wedding. A tart if ever he saw one.

Snivelling into her handkerchief and answering counsel's questions in a voice so low that the judge had to ask her to speak up. Yes, she had agreed to lend Eileen the flat on Friday nights. She and her husband went every Friday to visit his parents at Southend. They always left as soon as he shut the shop. No, her husband didn't know of the arrangement. She had given Mrs Morrisey the spare key without consulting him. There wasn't any other spare key that she knew of. Why had she done it? She was sorry for Eileen. Eileen had pressed her. She didn't think the Morriseys had much of a life together.

Here the judge interposed gently that the witness should confine herself to answering counsel's questions. She turned to him. 'I was only trying to help Eileen, my Lord.'

Then there was the letter. It was passed to the snivelling woman in the box, and she confirmed that it had been written to her by Mrs Morrisey. Slowly it was collected by the clerk and borne majestically across to counsel, who proceeded to read it aloud:

Dear Brenda,

We shall be at the flat on Friday after all. I thought I'd better let you know in case you and Ted changed your plans. But it will definitely be for the last time. George is getting suspicious, and I must think of the children. I always knew it would have to end. Thank you for being such a pal.

Eileen

The measured, upper-class voice ceased. Looking across at the jury, counsel laid the letter slowly down. The judge bent his head and made another notation. There was a moment of silence in the court. Then the witness was dismissed.

And so it went on. There was the paper seller at the end of Moulton Street who remembered Speller buying an *Evening Standard* just before eight o'clock. The accused was carrying a bottle under his arm and seemed very cheerful. He had no doubt his customer was the accused.

There was the publican's wife from the Rising Sun at the junction of Moulton Mews and High Street who testified that she served the prisoner with a whisky shortly before half past eight. He hadn't stayed long. Just long enough to drink it down. He had seemed very upset. Yes, she was quite sure it was the accused. There was a motley collection of customers to confirm her evidence. Gabriel wondered why the prosecution had bothered to call them, until he realised that Speller had denied visiting the Rising Sun, had denied that he had needed a drink.

There was George Edward Morrisey, described as an estate agent's clerk, thin-faced, tight-lipped, standing rigidly in his best blue serge suit. He testified that his marriage had been happy, that he had known nothing. His wife had told him that she spent Friday evenings learning to make pottery at LCC evening classes. The court tittered. The judge frowned.

In reply to counsel's questions, Morrisey said that he had stayed at home to look after the children. They were still a little young to be left alone at night. Yes, he had been at home the night his wife was killed. Her death was a great grief to him. Her liaison with the accused had come as a terrible shock. He spoke the word 'liaison' with an angry contempt, as if it were bitter on his tongue. Never once did he look at the prisoner.

There was the medical evidence – sordid, specific, but mercifully clinical and brief. The deceased had been raped, then stabbed three times through the jugular vein. There was the evidence of the accused's employer, who contributed a vague and imperfectly substantiated story about a missing meat skewer. There was the prisoner's landlady, who testified that he had arrived home on the night of the murder in a distressed state and that he had not got up to go to work next morning. Some of the threads were thin. Some, like the evidence of the butcher, obviously bore little weight even in the eyes of the prosecution. But together they were weaving a rope strong enough to hang a man.

The defending counsel did his best, but he had the desperate air of a man who knows that he is foredoomed to lose. He called witnesses to testify that Speller was a gentle, kindly boy, a generous friend, a good son and brother. The jury believed them. They also believed that he had killed his mistress. He called the accused. Speller was a poor witness, unconvincing, inarticulate. It would have helped, thought Gabriel, if the boy had shown some sign of pity for the dead woman. But he was too absorbed in his own danger to spare a thought for anyone else. Perfect fear casteth out love, thought Gabriel. The aphorism pleased him.

The judge summed up with scrupulous impartiality, treating the jury to an exposition on the nature and value of circumstantial evidence and an interpretation of the expression 'reasonable doubt'. The jury listened with respectful attention. It was impossible to guess what went on behind those twelve pairs of watchful, anonymous eyes. But they weren't out long.

Within forty minutes of the court rising, they were back, the prisoner reappeared in the dock, the judge asked the formal question. The foreman gave the expected answer, loud and clear. 'Guilty, my Lord.' No one seemed surprised.

The judge explained to the prisoner that he had been found guilty of the horrible and merciless killing of the woman who had loved him. The prisoner, his face taut and ashen, stared wild-eyed at the judge, as if only half hearing. The sentence was pronounced, sounding doubly horrible spoken in those soft judicial tones. Gabriel looked with interest for the black cap and saw with surprise and some disappointment that it was merely a square of some black material perched incongruously atop the judge's wig. The jury was thanked. The judge collected his notes like a businessman clearing his desk at the end of a busy day. The court rose. The prisoner was taken below. It was over.

The trial caused little comment at the office. No one knew that Gabriel had attended. His day's leave 'for personal reasons' was accepted with as little interest as any previous absence. He was too solitary, too unpopular, to be included in office gossip. In his dusty and ill-lit office, insulated by tiers of filing cabinets, he was the object of vague dislike or, at best, of a pitying tolerance. The filing room had never been a centre for cosy office chat. But he did hear the opinion of one member of the firm.

On the day after the trial, Mr Bootman, newspaper in hand, came into the general office while Gabriel was distributing the morning mail. 'I see they've disposed of our little local trouble,' Mr Bootman said. 'Apparently the fellow is to hang. A good thing too. It seems to have been the usual sordid story of illicit passion and general stupidity. A very commonplace murder.'

No one replied. The office staff stood silent, then stirred into life. Perhaps they felt that there was nothing more to be said.

It was shortly after the trial that Gabriel began to dream. The dream, which occurred about three times a week, was always the same. He was struggling across a desert under a blood-red sun, trying to reach a distant fort. He could sometimes see the fort clearly, although it never got any closer. There was an inner courtyard crowded with people, a silent black-clad multitude whose faces were all turned towards a central platform. On the platform was a gallows. It was a curiously elegant gallows, with two sturdy posts at either side and a delicately curved crosspiece from which the noose dangled.

The people, like the gallows, were not of this age. It was a Victorian crowd, the women in shawls and bonnets, the men in top hats or narrow-brimmed bowlers. He could see his mother there, her thin face peaked under the widow's veil. Suddenly she began to cry, and as she cried, her face changed and became the face of the weeping woman at the trial. Gabriel longed desperately to reach her, to comfort her. But with every step he sank deeper into the sand.

There were people on the platform now. One, he knew, must be the prison governor, top-hatted, frock-coated, bewhiskered, and grave. His clothes were those of a Victorian gentleman, but his face, under that luxuriant beard, was the face of Mr Bootman. Beside him stood the chaplain, in gown and bands, and on either side were two warders, their dark jackets buttoned high to their necks.

Under the noose stood the prisoner. He was wearing breeches and an open-necked shirt, and his neck was as white and delicate as a woman's. It might have been that other neck, so slender it looked. The prisoner was gazing across the desert towards Gabriel, not with desperate appeal but with great sadness in his eyes. And, this time, Gabriel knew that he had to save him, had to get there in time.

But the sand dragged at his aching ankles, and although he called that he was coming, coming, the wind, like a furnace blast, tore the words from his parched throat. His back, bent almost double, was blistered by the sun. He wasn't wearing a coat. Somehow, irrationally, he was worried that his coat was missing, that something had happened to it that he ought to remember.

As he lurched forward, floundering through the gritty morass, he could see the fort shimmering in the heat haze. Then it began to recede, getting fainter and farther, until at last it was only a blur among the distant sandhills. He heard a high, despairing scream from the courtyard – then awoke to know that it was his voice and that the damp heat on his brow was sweat, not blood.

In the comparative sanity of the morning, he analysed the dream and realised that the scene was one pictured in a Victorian news-sheet which he had once seen in the window of an antiquarian bookshop. As he remembered, it showed the execution of William Corder for the murder of Maria Marten in the red barn. The remembrance comforted him. At least he was still in touch with the tangible and sane world.

But the strain was obviously getting him down. It was time to put his mind to his problem. He had always had a good mind, too good for his job. That, of course, was why the other staff resented him. Now was the time to use it. What, exactly, was he worrying about? A woman had been murdered. Whose fault had it been? Weren't there a number of people who shared the responsibility?

That blonde tart, for one, who had lent them the flat. The husband, who had been so easily fooled. The boy, who had enticed her away from her duty to husband and children. The victim herself – particularly the victim. The wages of sin are death. Well, she had taken her wages now. One man hadn't been enough for her.

Gabriel pictured again that dim shadow against the bedroom curtains, the raised arms as she drew Speller's head down to her breast. Filthy. Disgusting. Dirty. The adjectives smeared his mind. Well, she and her lover had taken their fun. It was right that both of them should pay for it. He, Ernest Gabriel, wasn't concerned. It had only been by the merest chance that he had seen them from that upper window, only by chance that he had seen Speller knock and go away again.

Justice was being served. He had sensed its majesty, the beauty of its essential rightness, at Speller's trial. And he, Gabriel, was a part of it. If he spoke now, an adulterer might even go free. His duty was clear. The temptation to speak had gone forever.

It was in this mood that he stood with the small silent crowd outside the prison on the morning of Speller's execution. At the first stroke of eight, he, like the other men present, took off his hat.

Staring up at the sky high above the prison walls, he felt

again the warm exultation of his authority and power. It was on his behalf, it was at his, Gabriel's, bidding that the nameless hangman inside was exercising his dreadful craft ...

But that was sixteen years ago. Four months after the trial the firm, expanding and conscious of the need for a better address, had moved from Camden Town to north London. Gabriel had moved with it. He was one of the few people on the staff who remembered the old building. Clerks came and went so quickly nowadays; there was no sense of loyalty to the job.

When Gabriel retired at the end of the year, only Mr Bootman and the porter would remain from the old Camden Town days. Sixteen years. Sixteen years of the same job, the same bed-sitting room, the same half-tolerant dislike on the part of the staff. But he had had his moment of power. He recalled it now, looking round the small sordid sitting room with its peeling wallpaper, its stained boards. It had looked different sixteen years ago.

He remembered where the sofa had stood, the very spot where she had died. He remembered other things – the pounding of his heart as he made his way across the asphalt; the quick knock; the sidling through the half-opened door before she could realise it wasn't her lover; the naked body cowering back into the sitting room; the taut white throat; the thrust with his filing bodkin that was as smooth as puncturing soft rubber. The steel had gone in so easily, so sweetly.

And there was something else which he had done to her. But that was something it was better not to remember. And afterwards he had taken the bodkin back to the office, holding it under the tap in the washroom until no spot of blood could have remained. Then he had replaced it in his desk drawer with half a dozen identical others. There had been nothing to distinguish it any more, even to his eyes.

It had all been so easy. The only blood had been a gush on his right cuff as he withdrew the bodkin. And he had burned the coat in the office furnace. He still recalled the blast on his face as he thrust it in, and the spilled cinders like sand under his feet.

There had been nothing left to him but the key of the flat. He had seen it on the sitting-room table and had taken it away with him. He drew it now from his pocket and compared it with the key from the estate agent, laying them side by side on his outstretched palm. Yes, they were identical. They had had another one cut, but no one had bothered to change the lock.

He stared at the key, trying to recall the excitement of those weeks when he had been both judge and executioner. But he could feel nothing. It was all so long ago. He had been fifty then; now he was sixty-six. It was too old for feeling. And then he recalled the words of Mr Bootman. It was, after all, a very commonplace murder.

On Monday morning the girl in the estate office, clearing the mail from the letter box, called to the manager.

'That's funny! The old chap who took the key to the Camden Town flat has returned the wrong one. This hasn't got our label on it. Unless he pulled it off. Cheek! But why would he do that?'

She took the key over to the manager's desk, dumping his pile of letters in front of him. He glanced at it casually.

'That's the right key, anyway – it's the only one of that type we still have. Probably the label worked loose and fell off. You should put them on more carefully.'

'But I did!' Outraged, the girl wailed her protest. The manager winced.

'Then label it again, put it back on the board, and for God's sake don't fuss, that's a good girl.'

She glanced at him again, ready to argue. Then she shrugged. Come to think of it, he had always been a bit odd about that Camden Town flat.

'OK, Mr Morrisey,' she said.

The Hours of Darkness

Edmund Crispin

1

At ten thirty-five p.m. on Christmas Eve, Noel Carter said to Janice Mond:

'This is perfectly senseless, Janice. What does it matter if we *are* discovered?'

'If you're going to play a game at all, Noel,' said Janice sententiously, 'you must play it properly.'

'I didn't ask to play the damned game. Anyway, it's obviously unfair to be hiding outside the house – quite apart from the fact that we shall both be laid low with pneumonia in a few hours. Good heavens, Janice, it's freezing. I don't know how you can stand it. You've got practically nothing on.'

'You ought to be very pleased,' Janice replied coolly. 'After all, Noel, the sole purpose of playing hide-and-seek is to allow people to make love in decent privacy for a few minutes. Nothing will make me believe that Duncan is actually *looking* for anyone.'

'I wish he'd find us,' said Noel unchivalrously. 'I wish he'd find us and take us back to the fire. I should like some whisky. I wish you were a salamander.'

Janice sighed, but made no remark. Noel got up and went to the door of the little summer house, from which he surveyed the black bulk of Rydalls looming against a starlit but moonless sky, and the thin sheet of snow, marked only with their own footprints, which stretched bleakly in every direction. A small but chilling wind was moving among the bare branches of the trees in the park, and the only sound was the distant howling of a dog. It rose and fell on the night air with a monotonous persistency which became, after a few minutes, extremely trying.

'Dogs only make that noise,' Noel observed, 'when there are vampires leaving their graves.'

'Come and make love to me, Noel,' said Janice from the gloom at the back of the summer house.

'Darling, I should love to,' said Noel carefully, 'if it weren't for the fact that my animal heat – which, I may say, is always rather precarious – has now quite deserted me ... How much longer do we have to stay in this detestable hovel?'

Janice felt in her handbag and produced a tiny gold cigarette lighter. Its wavering flame lit up her ash-blonde hair and her pretty, petulant, childish features. She could not, thought Noel, be more than twenty. She looked at her wristwatch, a tiny, jewelled rectangle on her slender wrist.

'Ten minutes,' she announced. 'Then they'll ring the gong, and we can go back, and you can have your damned whisky.' She paused, and then said:

'You don't approve of me, do you, Noel?'

'I think you're very attractive indeed,' he answered – with truth, since the lighter was gleaming on her slim and gently rounded body in its white slipper satin gown, and her bare arms were smooth and soft to look at.

'Then why don't you make love to me?'

'Because' – the remark sounded a trifle priggish – 'I just don't make love to every pretty girl I happen to meet.'

'Why not?' she asked disconcertingly.

'I have principles,' Noel replied mendaciously. As a matter of fact he had none.

'You mean you're terrified of getting involved.'

'Very well.' Noel was annoyed at so much perceptivity. 'I'm terrified of getting involved. Also, I'm cold.'

'You needn't worry,' said Janice, with all the scorn of her youth. 'I shan't run after you ... Damn, this thing's getting hot—'

The lighter fell with a clatter on to the uneven wooden floor of the summer house. They were in darkness again. Noel dutifully groped about for it.

'I suppose the fact is,' Janice resumed in implausibly casual tones, 'that you're interested in Patricia.'

'Here's your lighter.'

'Thanks. Of course I don't blame you. Patricia's a very attractive girl, though I must say, I wish she wouldn't use that particular shade of lipstick.'

'Puss, puss.'

'Oh, don't be childish, Noel ... I wonder who it was attacked her the other night?'

They heard a car coming up the drive, its tyres crackling in the frozen snow. The dog gave one last, devastating howl, and then was mercifully silent. When the ignition of the car was turned off, it was possible to hear the high, metallic singing of the telephone wires in the road beyond the low flint wall which bounded the little estate. A freezing gust of wind blew through the summer-house door; Noel shivered.

'A servant, I suppose,' he replied. 'Apparently it was just an ordinary attempt at petty thieving. If Patricia hadn't rushed in and tried to apply ju-jitsu, she wouldn't have got hurt at all.'

'Anyway, I've taken to locking my door at night.'

'Wise girl,' Noel commented ironically. 'But I shouldn't worry. A repetition's not very likely. Besides, nothing valuable was taken.'

'The diary.'

'I don't believe Patricia ever had a diary ... Oh, what a comfortable way to spend Christmas Eve this is.'

'Will you please put your arms round me, Noel? I'm cold ... Lord, that can't be the gong, can it?' Janice sounded distinctly peevish. 'It's five minutes early.'

However, it was undoubtedly the gong. 'I'll tell you why it's early,' said Noel. 'They're making a last attempt to snatch us back from the jaws of the grave.'

'Race you to the front door.'

'You can't race in an evening dress. You'll fall.'

'I'll hold my skirt up. Come on.'

'How you would have enjoyed living in Sparta,' Noel remarked.

But Janice, with a finely feminine contempt for the laws of sport, had already left the summer house and was running across the white expanse of lawn. A little slip of moon was rising above the trees of the park. Its light was just sufficient to give precision to the outline of Rydalls and to evoke a watery, answering gleam from the bonnet of the car which stood, some hundreds of yards distant, below the steps of the terrace.

Sighing deeply, Noel exerted himself to follow.

He ran clumsily, for his feet were so cold that he could hardly feel them, but he succeeded, nonetheless, in catching Janice up just as she rounded the corner of the house by the billiard room. Lights flashed out from many of the windows; evidently the game was well and truly over. Giggling noisily, they panted up the terrace steps. These were dangerous, for the snow had hardened into a slippery, irregular surface; and Noel, cursing vehemently, nearly fell down on his face as he climbed them. They came in view of the windows of the long gallery.

'Look, Noel,' Janice gasped, catching him suddenly by the arm. 'Isn't – isn't that sweet?'

Secure in the conviction that Janice had only stopped the race because she knew she was going to lose it, Noel looked.

The long gallery was dimly illuminated by a lamp at the far end, where a door led into a vestibule giving on to the main hall; but in an alcove beyond the window at which they were standing a man and a woman were embracing beneath a branch of mistletoe. The man had his back to them, and since a dinner jacket, in a dinner-jacketed party, provides a very respectable form of anonymity, they were quite unable to make out who he was.

'But the girl's Louise,' Janice whispered.

'Louise?'

'Louise Munro. I know by the jade bracelet she's wearing.'
A note of indignation came into Janice's voice. 'I must say,
she's being very languid about it all.'

'Well, don't stand and stare at them. It's a perversion.'

'A perversion?'

'Called mixoscopy. Come in and get warm.' They walked
on to the front door.

'Kiss me, Noel,' said Janice.

'If you'll promise to come inside immediately afterwards.'

'Of course I promise.'

Noel found it a disturbingly pleasant kiss. Janice knew
this, and he knew that she knew. The whole thing, he
reflected, was distinctly a defeat for him.

'Now you must keep your promise,' he said.

'Of course, Noel,' Janice replied demurely.

2

The drawing room, when they reached it, was crowded; virtually the whole party had returned there at the conclusion
of the game, and Noel and Janice seemed to be the last to
arrive. Their host, Duncan MacAdam, approached them.
He was a man of about forty, tall, slim, and immaculately
dressed, with prematurely greying hair, the attractive accent
of an educated Scot, and a mobile, expressive, rather plump
face. He appeared to have money in his own right, and he
had bought Rydalls seven years previously. He lived as comfortably as governmental extortions permitted, and spent
the greater part of his time in giving house parties. In fact
they ran almost non-stop at Rydalls, for MacAdam's circle
of acquaintance was large. Yet he seemed to have no intimate

friends, and no woman – though many had tried – had, as yet, succeeded in marrying him.

'You've been outside,' he said accusingly. 'That constitutes cheating.'

'I told you,' said Noel to Janice.

'Anyway, Duncan,' Janice returned, 'I don't believe *you* attempted to find anyone.'

MacAdam grinned. 'I found Murchison,' he said, 'who was rather inadequately concealed at the sideboard, and betraying his presence by swilling noises. After that, I admit, I didn't get much further.'

'Why the sudden recall?'

MacAdam grinned again. 'Sorry if it disturbed you. A new guest arrived *in medias res*. Poor fellow, he was a bit distressed at finding the whole house in darkness. I think it must have reminded him of *The Travelling Grave* – you remember?'

'Who is it?' Noel asked. 'Anyone I know?'

'Peter Hadow.'

'The man who writes detective novels?'

'Yes. Come and meet him.'

'Can we meet him somewhere in front of the fire?'

'Of course. You must be frozen. Come along.'

They pushed through the chattering groups of guests towards a huge edifice of flaming logs. The room was brilliantly lighted by two electric chandeliers and a profusion of standard lamps. It was in the Queen Anne part of the house, tall, long, panelled in pine, and richly ornamented on the overmantel, the cornice and the pediment above the door; but the furniture was modern throughout. 'I possess no aesthetic sense,' MacAdam was accustomed to say, 'but my bodily perceptions are very acute ... Properly sprung chairs I must have.'

Peter Hadow was talking to Patricia Davenant and Richard Neame. For a specialist in the macabre he looked remarkably jumpy. He was a man of about thirty-five, precise to the point of pedantry in his speech, with an untidy mop of dark hair, a long, thin, enquiring nose, and small, weak blue eyes. He held a glass in one hand, and with the other tapped his pince-nez, in a fidgety manner, against a waistcoat button.

The courtesies were observed; conventional enquiries as to health conventionally disposed of; an antiphonal commentary on the weather and the state of the roads duly accomplished. MacAdam departed to fetch drinks for Noel and Janice.

'Patricia dear,' said Janice, 'what *have* you been doing to your dress?'

'I must go and deal with it,' Patricia Davenant answered. She was a tall and lovely girl, with a splendid head of red hair and a curiously ingenuous manner.

'No further trouble, I hope?' asked Noel.

Patricia smiled and shook her head. 'Just an accident. My shoulder strap broke.'

She was holding the dress hunched up under her left arm. 'I'd better change.'

'Patricia dear, you look charmingly like a Maenad,' said MacAdam, returning with the drinks. 'But as the male element of this party is remarkable rather for modesty than for brains, you're embarrassing everyone. Would you like to be lent a safety pin?'

Richard Neame frowned perceptibly.

Patricia giggled. 'No, thanks. I'll get out of the wretched frock altogether. Excuse me.' She left the room and went upstairs.

'You won't' – Peter Hadow turned to MacAdam – 'you won't of course inform the young lady of my reason for wishing to meet her? Or say anything about the book?'

'Certainly not,' MacAdam agreed; there was a twinkle in his eye. 'The young lady,' he explained to the others, 'is Louise. She was tied up with the Forrest case just before the war – or rather her brother was. Peter based one of his novels on it, and wants to talk to her.'

'You know the book?' Peter Hadow enquired.

'Oh, yes,' said Noel and Janice simultaneously. 'Oh, certainly.'

'Splendid.' Hadow appeared pleased. 'Of course, it isn't published yet,' he added gently. 'There were certain difficulties about libel.'

'It was a murder case, wasn't it?' said Richard Neame. He was a rather colourless man of about thirty-five who was engaged to marry Patricia Davenant. 'Will she want to talk about it?'

'That,' said MacAdam, 'is the problem. Don't for heaven's sake upset the girl, Peter.'

'If she doesn't offer to talk about it,' Hadow assured him, 'I'll drop the whole thing ... Can you point her out to me, by the bye?'

MacAdam craned his neck to look round the room. 'She doesn't appear to be in here.'

'She was in the long gallery when we came in,' said Janice,

'and I suppose may be there still. There was a man with her,' Janice added rather primly.

'This house seems to be a temple to Aphrodite Pandemos,' MacAdam observed. 'Well, I've no doubt she'll turn up sooner or later ... Weren't we going to play charades?'

'I'm very good at charades,' Hadow announced unexpectedly, 'so you must put me in charge of one of the sides. But I think I'd better get my car under cover first.'

'Oh, I've told someone to deal with that,' said MacAdam. 'Have another drink, and then I'll show you your room, and then we can make a start. I don't suppose anyone has the least desire to play charades, but I refuse to allow dancing to begin until midnight.'

A quarter of an hour later he was issuing instructions to the party at large – with the exception, that is, of four people who had pleaded age and lack of histrionic ability and had slunk off into the library to play bridge. The party responded with cries of not unmixed enthusiasm.

'And by the way,' said MacAdam, 'it scarcely seems to me that we're all here. Isn't Patricia back yet?'

'Give her a chance,' said Richard Neame. 'You know how long women take over these things.'

'And where is Louise?' MacAdam's plump face grew comical with dismayed enquiry. 'Has anyone seen Louise?'

No one, apparently, had seen Louise since before the game of hide-and-seek.

'But you might check up on the men,' Noel suggested *sotto voce*. He was rather surprised when, in the event, all of them were accounted for.

'We'd better look in the long gallery,' said Janice. 'I hope she isn't ill, or anything.'

A voluntary search party left the drawing room. It consisted of Noel, Janice, MacAdam, Peter Hadow, Richard Neame and a middle-aged man named Simon Moore, who was correctly assumed by everyone to be trying to marry Louise Munro for her money. They crossed the hall, with its broad, green-carpeted staircase, passed through the vestibule and entered the long gallery.

It was the least used room in the house, but its size and its polished floor made it eminently suitable for dancing. Consequently there was little furniture in it at this time, apart from a tiny improvised bar, a large radiogram, and rows of chairs against the walls. The standard lamp by the door was still on, but blue velvet curtains had been drawn across the windows. Their footsteps echoed a little as they walked up to the far end.

MacAdam was ahead of the others. They saw him stop abruptly as he reached the alcove, and heard him utter a stifled exclamation. Louise Munro had always been considered an attractive woman, but strangulation and a blood-soaked body are not calculated to enhance anyone's charms.

3

Some fifteen miles away, in the North Oxford home of the university Professor of English Language and Literature, a children's party was in progress.

Its host was seated, glowering, at one end of the drawing room. He was attempting, simultaneously, to construct a crane out of Meccano, drink a glass of whisky, and keep off a small and solemn-looking girl whose pleasure it seemed to be to buffet him disinterestedly about the ears. His clean-shaven face was ruddy with effort, and his brown hair stood up in spikes from the crown of his head. A few feet away from him, an aged colleague named Wilkes was engaged in improvising a rather lurid and improbable fairy story.

'Heh,' he was saying. 'So the wicked queen left the mirror and ran through the corridors of the great castle, and came to the huge deserted kitchen. And in the floor of the kitchen there was a heavy trapdoor bound with rusty iron hinges. So the wicked queen lifted the trapdoor and climbed down the damp and slimy steps into the dark dungeons. Heh.'

'Sounds corny to me,' said a rather unpleasant boy.

'What was it like in the dungeons?' asked a saccharine little girl with a blue bow in her hair.

'It was ruddy awful,' said Wilkes ill-advisedly.

'Ruddy awful,' screamed the children in chorus. 'It was ruddy awful.'

In the hall outside, the telephone could be heard ringing. Mrs Fen, a pleasant, plain, bespectacled woman, came in and approached her eccentric husband.

'Gervase,' she said, 'you're wanted.'

'Thank God for that,' said Fen, wiping his brow. The crane by now somewhat resembled a skyscraper in course of demolition by high explosive. 'Look here, it's late. Oughtn't all these children to go home?'

'We'll send them away,' said his wife soothingly, 'when Dr Wilkes has finished his story.'

'Ah,' said Fen. He rose to his feet. An aeroplane driven by elastic sailed across the room and caught him a glancing blow on the left temple. A freckled child of indeterminate sex had got hold of his whisky. Leaving his wife to deal with the situation, he beat a hasty retreat.

'Well?' he said into the telephone. 'Fen here.'

'This is Dick Freeman,' said the Chief Constable of Oxford from his house on Boar's Hill.

'Oh, is it,' Fen replied affably. 'And a merry Christmas to you.'

'You're not sober,' said Sir Richard Freeman with some certainty.

'Well, don't you believe in celebrating Christmas, you puritanical old dullard?'

'No.'

'Every time you say that,' said Fen reproachfully, 'a fairy dies somewhere ... What do you want?'

'There's been a murder.'

'A scientist, one hopes.'

'No, a girl. I thought it might interest you to go along.'

'Where is it?'

But for the moment this information was not forthcoming. Heralded by a sound like a cork coming out of a bottle, a feminine voice of positively obscene gaiety enquired whether they had finished.

'No, I haven't,' said Sir Richard Freeman. 'I've hardly begun.'

'A merry Christmas to you.'

'Don't you cut me off,' said Sir Richard with sudden suspicion. 'I'm the Chief Constable. You can't cut *me* off. I'm the—'

There was a dull crackling, like thorns beneath a pot, and

then silence. Fen joggled the receiver-rest experimentally two or three times, and then replaced the instrument. From the drawing room, Wilkes could be heard banging about with the fire irons in an attempt to simulate rattling chains. The freckled child who had seized Fen's whisky was hurried by Mrs Fen through the hall into the cloakroom to be sick. In a few moments the telephone rang again.

'The house is called Rydalls,' said Sir Richard. 'At Sanford Angelorum. And if the blasted exchange cuts me off again I'll have them all by the ears.'

'Or lay them all by the heels, of course,' Fen suggested. 'Sanford Angelorum's a long way away.'

'You've got a car, haven't you?'

'Yes,' said Fen, brightening. 'So I have. Are you going to be there?'

'No. I'm off to bed.'

'Who's in charge?'

'A local man – by name Wyndham. I'll let him know you're coming.'

'That's the way,' said Fen approvingly. 'Sleep tight.'

He rang off, and went into the drawing room to announce his departure. It was accepted with indifference. A pugnacious little girl took a swipe at his leg, missed and toppled over. Her wails pursued him out of the house.

He drove to Rydalls in his small red sports car, which was named Lily Christine III, and sang loudly to keep out the cold. His voice mingled hideously with the voices of peregrinating bands of carol singers, woke sleeping dogs, and bedevilled the dreams of rustics.

4

There were already two police cars standing in the drive when he arrived at Rydalls. He was welcomed by Wyndham, an obese, gentle, worried-looking inspector of police, and taken into MacAdam's study, which was being used as an office. It was a small room compared with the others in the house, snug, well-to-do, and little suggestive, despite its broad, flat-topped desk, of any kind of work. Despite MacAdam's pretensions to Philistinism, the pictures on the walls showed a certain taste.

'It's a mess, sir,' said Wyndham without further preliminary. He had an unexpectedly high, piping voice. 'And a cruel mess at that.'

'Who was the girl?'

'A Mrs Louise Munro. Youngish, it seems – somewhere in the late twenties, I should say, though no one seems to have any clear idea about her age. Her husband died in a flying accident during the war, when they hadn't been married more than six months. A much older man, I understand, and very well-off ... Would you like to see the body? It's still on the spot, though we shall have to move it soon.'

'Right. You lead the way.'

They left the study and crossed the hall to the door of the vestibule which led into the long gallery, and which was guarded by a constable. The drawing-room door was ajar, and from it could be heard a subdued hum of conversation.

'Such a hell of a lot of them,' Wyndham commented gloomily. 'If I know anything about it, we shall be here half the night.'

The constable saluted. They entered the long gallery. A

man who had been bending over Louise Munro's body came to meet them. He was young and neatly dressed, with a long, earnest face and a Roman nose.

'Well, doctor?' said Wyndham.

'Thank God I don't see *that* sort of thing very often,' said the doctor. 'The cause of death was strangulation, I fancy – though that won't be certain until I get a look at the internal organs. She may simply have died of loss of blood.'

'H'm,' said Wyndham dubiously. 'Well, I don't suppose it matters very much.'

'The slashing must have been done when she was still alive,' the doctor went on. 'Otherwise she'd hardly have bled so much.'

'H'm,' said Wyndham again. He turned to Fen. 'Look at that, sir. I suppose the killer thought she was dead when he started his butchering.'

The body of Louise Munro lay on its back. She had been a tall, dark-haired, slender girl; and a dispassionate consideration of her face, even in death, might have seen there signs of weakness and indecision. The features were distorted to a hideous mask; the eyes were bulging; the flesh was cyanosed and swollen; and there were traces of bloodstained froth at the nose and mouth.

Wyndham bent and turned the body over. The black evening gown had left her back naked to the waist, and the soft white skin was now scarred with a dozen long, deep cuts, on which the blood was clotted and black. Indeed, there seemed to be blood everywhere on the body and on the floor round it.

'Yes,' said Fen, almost to himself, 'someone disliked that

young woman very much ... This is one of those occasions when the thought of judicial hanging gives me a positive pleasure. Is there anything else I ought to see?'

'The gloves,' Wyndham replied, 'and the knife. They're over here.' He crossed to the mantelpiece and Fen followed him. 'Both smothered in blood, as you'd expect. They were on the floor by the body. It seems that the knife comes from the kitchen. There are no prints on it. And no name in the gloves, which seem to be quite ordinary.'

Fen nodded. He had cast no more than a cursory glance at the exhibits. 'She was throttled?' he enquired.

'I think so. What's your opinion, doctor?'

'Almost certainly,' said the doctor. 'The bruising's distinctive.'

'Well, sir,' said Wyndham, 'if there's nothing else, I think we might have her taken away. Has the ambulance arrived, doctor?'

'It's just come, I think,' said the doctor, who was peering between the curtains. 'But there's a beastly little red sports car in the way of it.'

'Beastly?' said Fen indignantly. 'There's nothing beastly about Lily Christine. Still, I suppose I'd better go and move her.'

When he returned to the house, Wyndham was talking to a police sergeant in the hall.

'First of all, find out who has alibis for that game of hide-and-seek and who hasn't,' he was saying. 'And then when you've brought me the list you'd better go and search the girl's bedroom ... Oh, and send' – he pulled out a notebook and consulted it – 'Noel Carter and Janice Mond to me in the study.'

As they returned there: 'Hide-and-seek?' said Fen interrogatively.

'It happened during a game,' Wyndham explained, 'which of course means a general lack of alibi ... The girl wasn't dead when they found her, you know.'

'Not dead?' Fen was startled. 'Oh, my dear paws. Was she conscious?'

'Yes, and said a few words. Nothing very revealing, though.' They had reached the study, and Wyndham lowered his considerable bulk with obvious relief into a chair. 'I'll get this fellow Carter to run over it for you.'

'Who's he?'

'Just one of the guests – a young man. He has an unassuming air and a good deal of basic conceit. Also he's rather more fussy and old-maidish than suits his years, but I think he's all right, and he appears to have a definite alibi.'

'And the girl – Janice somebody?'

'She was with him all through the game. They were canoodling in a summer house.'

'Good God.' Fen was shocked. 'In this weather?'

'I know. Still, there are the Esquimaux, of course. I often wonder how they manage.'

'Igloos are very warm, I believe,' said Fen, interested.

'Yes.' Wyndham abandoned this topic with evident reluctance. 'Anyway, she's a forward little minx. *And* got her hooks in him. The more I see of women looking for husbands,' he added thoughtfully, 'the more I'm convinced of the total unscrupulousness of the sex.'

There was a knock at the door, and Noel and Janice came in. Fen noted with interest that the girl was considerably more at ease than the man, though both were a little pale. Wyndham motioned them to sit down.

'I'm sorry we have to trouble you again,' he said. 'But Professor Fen is interested in this business, and I think it would be a good thing if he heard your part of it in your own words.'

Noel shrugged. 'That's perfectly all right by me. You know, we've tried and tried, but neither of us has the least idea who that man was we saw. It can't have been someone from outside, I suppose?'

Wyndham shook his head grimly. 'We've checked on wheel marks and footprints in the snow, Mr Carter. The only wheel marks are those of Mr Hadow's car, the only footprints are yours and Miss Mond's, to and from the summer house.'

'So that's that,' said Janice, absently twisting a sapphire ring on her finger. 'Our old friend, the Closed Circle.' Unexpectedly, she shivered. 'Thank God Noel and I are out of it. You don't suspect us of collusion, do you, Inspector?'

'I don't suspect anyone of anything at the moment, Miss Mond,' Wyndham answered evasively. 'Now, Mr Carter: you and Miss Mond were recalled from the summer house by a pre-arranged signal – the ringing of the gong. That was at 10.40, wasn't it?'

'Yes. It was five minutes earlier than we expected. Hadow arrived, and Duncan – that's MacAdam – brought the game to a premature stop.'

'And you heard Mr Hadow drive up to the door?'
'Yes.'

'This isn't the detective novelist, is it?' Fen interrupted.
'Apparently, sir, yes.'

'Admirable,' Fen murmured. 'I've always wanted to meet him. *The King of the Groves* is almost as frightening a book as *The Burning Court*, and I can't say better than that ... Sorry. Go on.'

Wyndham said: 'Then you must have arrived outside the windows of the long gallery at about 10.41?'

'I suppose so.' Noel frowned, without apparent reason. 'And were confronted with the spectacle of the murderer kissing the murderee under the mistletoe ...'

'Noel,' said Janice with sudden urgency, 'I've only just thought ... She must have been ... That is, he must have started by then ... I remember saying she looked very languid. Oh, God,' Janice concluded in a small voice.

'I don't see,' Noel protested, 'why it shouldn't have happened after we went away ... Were we the last to get back to the drawing room? It would seem to depend on that.'

'I'll check on it, sir,' said the inspector. 'It may narrow down the times a little. Or again it may not. That kiss you saw could have been a perfectly innocent affair, with the girl alive and well. There's no reason, on the evidence, why the murder shouldn't have been committed *afterwards*.'

'But who by? We were all in the draw— Oh, hell. No, we weren't, though.'

Wyndham looked at him sharply, and tapped his pencil on the arm of his chair. 'Can you remember who was *not* in the drawing room, Mr Carter – between the end of the hide-and-seek game and the discovery of the body?'

'Yes. I think I can, that is. Patricia – that's Patricia Davenant – had broken a shoulder strap, and went up to her room to change. Then four of the older people got up a bridge game in the library – old Murchison and his wife, and Mr and Mrs Joyce. I imagine, though, that they must have been together all the time. And Duncan went to show Peter Hadow his room. But damn it all, it would have been abnormally risky at that time. And what would Louise have been doing, alone in the long gallery?'

'Waiting for someone, perhaps,' Janice suggested. 'And I suppose the assumption is that if the kiss we saw was a genuine innocuous affair, the man concerned is afraid to come forward after what's happened.'

Wyndham nodded. 'That's it, more or less. But I agree that the other notion's more plausible – namely, that the murderer heard you coming in the middle of his – activities, and snatched the girl up and kissed her – kissed her: my God, what a nerve – to put you off the scent. There's only one door to the long gallery, isn't there? – the one that leads through the vestibule into the hall? Well, then, if he'd just left her, and made for that, he would have been approaching the light and there would have been every chance of your recognising him ...'

'*Hey!*' Fen howled. There was an astonished silence. 'You seem to forget,' he went on waspishly, 'that I know nothing whatever about all this. You daze me, with your alternative hypotheses. Let me get the set-up clear. When you looked into the long gallery, the lights were on?'

'A light was on,' said Noel. 'A small standard lamp at the end by the door. The *other* end, of course, where the couple was standing, was almost dark.'

'And all the curtains were open?'

'Yes.'

Fen muttered something unintelligible, and lit a cigarette.

Then he went on: 'Doesn't it strike you as extraordinary that a murderer should go about his business in a lighted room – even a dimly lighted room – with the curtains wide; and the rest of the party pottering about anywhere and everywhere in and out of the house?'

'I don't think he can have expected anyone to be *outside*,' said Noel.

'And then, you see, the lights were all turned off for the game,' said Janice.

'At the main,' said Noel.

'And then when they were all turned on again—'

'Five minutes earlier than anyone expected.'

'—it must have taken him completely by surprise.'

'And he can't have missed hearing us coming.'

'The lights went on just as we rounded the corner of the house.'

'So you see—'

'Yes, just a minute, please,' said Fen, eyeing them somewhat askance. 'I think I've managed to grasp all that. Can't you say anything definite about the man?'

Noel sneezed, and gazed reproachfully at Janice, who refused to look at him. Through the folds of his handkerchief he mumbled:

'Well, he was wearing a dinner jacket; but so was every other male in the party.'

'His waistline certainly wasn't more than average,' Janice added, 'which cuts out one or two people. I don't know about the height. Average, I should say.'

'Yes,' said Noel. 'And his head was in shadow, so he might have been dark or fair.'

Fen asked: 'Could it have been a woman dressed as a man?'

They stared at him. 'I suppose so,' said Janice. 'But then there would have been no time to change back again. All the women in the party were present and correct when we got back to the drawing room – as far as I know, anyway.'

Fen turned to Wyndham. 'What about the servants?'

'They're out of it,' said Wyndham definitely. 'They went off duty at ten o'clock, and held a Christmas Eve celebration in their own sitting room. They were all together during the whole of the relevant time. Thank God one can narrow down the field that far.'

'Ah,' said Fen gnomically. He resumed his questions. 'When you left the window of the long gallery, you presumably didn't go straight back into the drawing room? If you had, you would have arrived before, or simultaneously with, the person who was with Mrs Munro.'

'No, we didn't go straight back,' said Noel.

'Noel insisted on kissing me outside the front door,' Janice explained with maidenly prevarication.

'Well, I'm damned,' said Noel, and sneezed again.

'Very proper,' Fen commented, beaming at them like some sentimental old aunt. 'And you saw no one in the hall when at last you did get inside?'

'No one.'

'What makes you so sure that the girl you saw in the long gallery *was* Louise Munro?

'Now I come to think of it, said Noel blankly, 'I'm not at all sure. In fact, it was Janice who said—'

'She was wearing Louise's jade bracelet, anyway,' Janice

interrupted. 'It caught the light. So obviously, I assumed it was Louise.'

The clock on the mantelpiece struck half past midnight, in tiny, fluid chimes.

'All right,' said Fen with a sigh. 'Now, about finding the unfortunate girl. What time would that be?'

'About five past eleven, I believe,' Noel replied. He lit a cigarette and sucked at it dispiritedly. 'Five of us went across to the long gallery. We were in that deplorably jocose condition which always seems to be induced by playing children's games.'

'Who were the five?'

'Janice, myself, Duncan, Richard Neame and Simon Moore.'

'Who are Richard Neame and Simon Moore?'

'Richard's a master at some derelict boys' school or other. Very stodgy and earnest about Education. Also, he's quite insanely in love with that little b-i-t-c-h Patricia Davenant, and engaged to marry her. Simon Moore's middle-aged, very hail-fellow-well-met, and a professional weekender. He wanted to marry Louise, but only for her money, I fancy.'

'It's a funny thing,' said Fen reminiscently. 'I always intended to marry some rich woman or other. But I never came across one,' he concluded with pathos. 'Well, well … Anyway, you were all together when you found Louise Munro.'

'Yes.' Noel absently stubbed out his cigarette, which he had hardly started to smoke, and lit another one. 'Janice let out a shriek like a startled gull—'

'Oh, don't be an idiot, Noel,' said Janice with exaggerated weariness.

'—and Duncan lifted Louise's head; she was lying on her back. He said: "She's still alive," and then she opened her eyes and looked at us, and Duncan asked her who – who was responsible. I don't think I shall ever forget the sounds she made when she tried to speak, and what she finally said.' Noel paused, soberly.

'Well?'

'She said: "Patricia ... in danger ... help her." And then she stopped, and Richard looked round like a startled rabbit, and scuttled off with Simon Moore to Patricia's bedroom. MacAdam said: "Tell us who did this," and Louise muttered – poor girl, she must have been in horrible pain: "Mustn't be destroyed ... I'll tell you ... who ..." And then she died.'

Noel put out the second cigarette. For a moment there was a silence. Fen broke it by asking:

'And what about this other girl – Patricia?'

'She was all right, but—' Noel turned to Wyndham. 'You know more about this part than I do.'

Wyndham stirred uneasily in his chair. 'Yes,' he said. 'It seems that Miss Davenant is in the habit of taking a tonic every night.' He paused, and added heavily: 'We found a large quantity of strychnine in it.'

5

Sergeant Stokes came in, and deposited a sheet of paper in front of the inspector. He was a ruddy, amiable young man.

'It's easier than we thought,' he announced. 'Only three men and one woman unaccounted for during the whole of the game. It would appear' – the sergeant grinned unprofessionally – 'that people hid, for the most part, in couples. Mr MacAdam and an old gentleman named Mr Murchison have partial alibis. They met about five minutes after the game started, and drank whisky by candlelight until Mr Hadow arrived. No one admits to having gone into the long gallery: they say it was too near and obvious a hiding place.'

Wyndham uttered a faint grunt. 'The body's been taken away?'

'Yes.'

'In that case you can transfer Scott from the door of the long gallery to me here. I shall want to interview some of these people. You'd better go now and search Mrs Munro's room.'

The sergeant vaguely parodied a salute, and departed. Wyndham read aloud from the paper on his knees.

'Patricia Davenant. Richard Neame. Simon Moore. Edgar Nathan. It seems they've none of them got alibis. Who's Edgar Nathan?'

'A ghastly man,' Noel explained obliquely. 'High church. Arty. Blue in the jowl.'

'And wearing a dinner jacket?' Fen put in.

'No. Clerical black … Oh, I see what you mean. Yes, from behind, and in a dim light, it would look like a dinner jacket.'

The constable who had been guarding the door of the long gallery came in.

'Sit down, Scott,' said Wyndham. 'I'll have something for you to do in a moment … Mr Carter, I suppose there's no doubt that Mrs Munro was all right immediately before the game of hide-and-seek?'

'No doubt whatever. I saw her myself.'

'Then there are two possibilities: either she was killed during the game, or she was killed in the interval between the end of the game and the time when she was found. Now: those without alibis for one or both of those periods are Patricia Davenant, Richard Neame, Simon Moore, Edgar Nathan, Duncan MacAdam and Peter Hadow. I include the last two on the assumption that MacAdam didn't stay with Hadow once he'd shown him up to his room. The bridge party I should think we could rule out. Is it *impossible* that either Neame, Moore or Nathan could have been the man you saw in the long gallery with Mrs Munro?'

'No,' said Noel immediately. 'It might have been any of them.'

'Was Mrs Munro the sort of person to allow virtually anyone to kiss her? I ask on the assumption that she was killed *after* the episode you witnessed.'

Janice had the grace to look uncomfortable. 'Yes, she was,' she said. 'Louise was quite promiscuous. I'm sorry if that sounds catty, but it happens to be true.'

Wyndham sighed. 'Thank you very much. Is there anything else you want to ask, Professor Fen?'

Fen, who had been fidgeting with a music box and had succeeded in inducing it to perform 'The Bluebells of Scotland', said:

'Yes, I've got two questions. First, are you sure Louise Munro wasn't raving when she said those few words after you found her?'

Noel hesitated, thinking back. 'No, I'm certain she wasn't,' he answered at last. 'I think she had something clear and definite and sane to say to us. Anyway, she was right about Patricia.'

'I quite agree,' said Janice with decision.

'And second,' said Fen, attempting to stop 'The Bluebells of Scotland' and failing, 'how long did you two stay kissing outside the front door?'

'Not more than two minutes,' Janice replied primly. 'I wouldn't allow it.'

Noel made an incoherent noise, and sneezed a third time.

'Well, I must drive you away,' said Wyndham. 'But I'd better have one or two details for my report before you go. Age, Mr Carter?'

'Twenty-seven.'

'Occupation?'

'Assyriology.'

'Scarcely very funny, is that, Mr Carter?'

'Independent means, then. But my hobby's Assyriology.' ('Cripes,' said Janice.)

'Age, Miss Mond?'

'Twenty.'

'Occupation?'

'Bright Young Person.' Janice grinned. 'Schoolgirl emeritus. Prospectively, Mrs Noel Carter.'

'Like hell!' said Noel, startled. They went out, arguing.

'Well, there we are,' said Wyndham with some satisfaction. 'That clears things up a little.'

With a savage rending of clockwork, 'The Bluebells of Scotland' came to an end. Fen hastily replaced the instrument on its table. 'Tell me about the strychnine,' he said.

'It's only an assumption as yet. But what ought to be an ordinary, watery tonic now tastes very bitter and unpleasant. Of course I shall have it analysed.'

'Strychnine.' Fen was thoughtful. 'Rather a silly poison to use: it can be detected so easily ... How did you come to find out about it?'

'It was that fellow Neame. He's daft about the girl Patricia. As far as I can make out, he spent about half an hour searching her room for spring-guns and whatnot, forbade her to leave his sight, and eventually thought of poisons and tasted this tonic. I could scarcely get a look at Mrs Munro for the fuss he was making about it when I arrived.'

Fen snorted. 'Well, *he* didn't try to poison her, that's certain. What do you propose doing now?'

'See these people without alibis, I should think. How about having MacAdam first?'

'Yes,' said Fen; and added hopefully: 'Since this house belongs to him, he might give us some whisky.'

6

This, in fact, was what MacAdam did; and Fen, restored to his normal good humour, punctuated the interview which followed with an unearthly rendering of 'I Saw Three Kings Go Sailing By'.

'I know there's something obscurely wrong about the words,' he admitted when remonstrated with. 'But the tune has always seemed to me a very nice one.'

MacAdam was undoubtedly worried; the lines of his plump, mobile face were as if graven into it. He held an unlighted cigar between his fingers, and his greying hair was slightly dishevelled. The duties of hospitality performed, he sat down as though exhausted, and said:

'Well?'

'A few gaps to fill in, Mr MacAdam,' said Wyndham cheerfully. 'I won't keep you longer than I can help.'

MacAdam gestured vaguely. 'That's all right. I should have been up most of the night, anyway. So would the others. Fire away.'

'In this game of hide-and-seek, you were – what's the technical term?'

'"He". I didn't do much looking, though.'

'Apparently not. Did the people concerned expect you to do any looking?'

'I shouldn't think so. The fact is, Inspector, that there are quite a number of young people in the party, and they'd got to the stage when they were looking amorously at one another and wondering how in God's name they could find an excuse to get away and spoon in a dark corner. So I gave them the excuse. I'm sure no one regarded the hiding-and-seeking very seriously.'

'The game began when?'

'At ten twenty-five. I set a strict time limit of twenty minutes – though in the event it was only fifteen.'

'You yourself turned off the lights?'

'Yes, from the main switch in the hall. I'd warned the servants about it, and provided them with candles. I'd also provided myself with a candle, I may say, as I didn't propose to sit about in darkness the whole time.'

'Where were you all when the game started?'

'Outside in the hall. When I said "Go" and turned the

lights off, there were the inevitable whispers and giggles and shrieks and people bumping into one another.

'Then in a minute or two they all made off, *tant bien que mal*, and I could hear old Murchison cursing like a trooper as he tried to find the whisky on the drawing-room sideboard. I lit my candle and chatted to him until Peter Hadow arrived. Poor fellow, he must have had a nasty turn when I opened the door for him; he probably thought that it was his last hour, and that they'd come for him with a coffin and tapers. Anyway, I set Murchison to belabour the gong, and then turned on the lights.'

'And people came back more or less at once?'

'Yes. I think that as the gong was early they must have thought there'd been some kind of accident.'

'You didn't see anyone emerge from the vestibule which leads into the long gallery?'

'No. I went straight back into the drawing room, as a matter of fact.'

'Can you remember in what order people returned?'

'Absolutely impossible, I'm afraid. I believe Simon Moore was *among* the first – I remember getting him a drink. And certainly Noel Carter and Janice Mond were last, because just before they arrived I'd been checking up to make sure everybody was there. But beyond that, I really can't say; obviously one wasn't paying much attention.'

'Thank you. And what then?'

'I introduced Janice and Noel to Peter Hadow. Patricia Davenant disappeared upstairs to fix her dress. And I took Peter to his room.'

'Did you stay with him?'

'No. I told him to come down when he was ready, and left him to it.'

'You returned to the drawing room immediately, then?'

'No again. I'd got somewhat grubby during the course of the evening, so I went to my own room for a wash.'

'That took you how long?'

'Oh … say ten minutes. Perhaps a little more.'

Wyndham paused for a moment to consider. Then said: 'As regards that knife that was used: I suppose unobserved access to the kitchen would be easy enough, wouldn't it?'

'After dinner was over and cleared away, yes. The servants have been having some sort of party in their own sitting room.'

'I see.' Wyndham began drawing mermaids on a blank page of his notebook. Fen hummed furtively. MacAdam lay back limply in his chair; the cigar which he held was still unlighted.

'How long have you known Mrs Munro?' Wyndham asked.

'About four years, on and off. I met her at a first night in town, just before she was married. We continued to run across one another, but this is the first time she's been down here. As a matter of fact, I really only invited her because Peter Hadow wanted a chance to meet her.'

'Why was that, sir?'

'It seems she was somehow connected with the Forrest murder case, just before the war.'

'*What?*' Fen sat up with such suddenness that he nearly knocked over the glass of whisky which was balanced precariously on the arm of his chair. He rescued it in time, however, and clasped it tenderly between his hands. 'What was her maiden name?'

'Benest, I think.'

'Oh, my fur and whiskers,' Fen exclaimed. He generally had recourse to the White Rabbit in moments of high excitement. 'Sorry. Go on.'

MacAdam looked curiously at him. '*I* can't go on, I'm afraid. I don't take any interest in these things, and I only know the case by name. Peter's the man to ask. He's got it all at his fingertips.'

Wyndham blew his nose. It was evident that his recollection of the trial in question was of the vaguest, and equally evident that he was not going to admit this in front of MacAdam. A premonitory rumbling in his throat suggested that some kind of evasive manoeuvre was in prospect, but whatever it was, Fen forestalled it.

'Can I make use of your constable for a moment?' he asked; and on Wyndham's assenting, hastily scribbled some names on a piece of paper, went to the door, opened it, and fetched in Scott, who was hovering about in the hall and was manifestly glad to be given something to do.

Fen handed him the paper and said: 'Will you go into the drawing room, please, and ask the guests collectively if any of them either knew *or had heard of* any of the people on this list before August, 1939? You'd better read out the names one by one, and make a note of whatever response there may be in each case.' He turned to Wyndham. 'Is that all right as far as you're concerned, Inspector?'

Wyndham nodded. 'But what are the names?' he enquired when Scott had gone.

'Simply your list of suspects,' said Fen, grinning. 'Sorry to interrupt you.'

'I haven't much more to ask,' Wyndham admitted. 'Mrs Munro was well-off, wasn't she, Mr MacAdam?'

'I believe so.'

'Do you happen to know who was her heir?'

'I don't at all.'

'Well, I do,' Fen interposed complacently. 'Or at all events, I have a shrewd idea. But more of that when we've heard what Hadow has to say. I've got a question, too. There must have been some kind of attack on Patricia Davenant previous to this evening's business, mustn't there?'

Wyndham glanced at him sharply. 'Had you been told about that?'

'No,' Fen countered with some indignation. 'I deduced it. What's the good of a detective if he doesn't deduce anything? But what exactly happened?'

MacAdam shrugged. 'Well, we've only her account of it. She came down two evenings ago looking a bit bruised and dishevelled, and said someone – she didn't know who, or whether it was a man or a woman – had been robbing her room, and had stolen her private diary. It seems that she went into her room to fetch something, and was tripped up and tumbled onto the floor before she had time to as much as put the light on. Apparently some kind of brief wrestling match ensued, but Patricia banged her head against the chest of drawers, and the other person was out of the room and away before she had a chance to recover.'

'Where were the other guests at this time?'

'They were unpacking in their rooms. That's really the

trouble. There was only Murchison and his wife and myself downstairs.'

'So it could have been any of them?'

'I suppose so.'

'What did you do about it?'

'What could I do about it?' MacAdam spread his hands in a gesture of humorous resignation. 'As far as was possible, I simply ignored the whole affair. Patricia wasn't really upset. She's far from being a hysterical type, and when she came to tell us about it, she was much more astonished than frightened. There wasn't any kind of clue ...'

'Nothing besides the diary was taken?'

'No ... Oh, but there was one odd thing. Patricia's typewriter had been opened, and I imagine used. Of course, poor old Richard was in a state of complete panic. He's utterly devoted to that girl.'

'And yet,' said Fen, 'they weren't together during the game of hide-and-seek.'

MacAdam smiled; he looked tired. 'That was due to a ridiculous quarrel earlier in the evening. Nothing important, of course – Richard, who is *sérieux*, raised some portentous objection to playing children's games, Patricia said he was pompous, and so it went on. Naturally, Richard became vastly repentant almost immediately afterwards, but Patricia snubbed him, in her own placid way, and he's been running about all evening looking like a whipped dog.' MacAdam chuckled.

'Just one more thing. Had Louise Munro been behaving in any way oddly since she arrived?'

'Oh, yes.' MacAdam was looking at them from narrowed

eyes. 'I think – in fact, I'm certain – that she was frightened of something. Or someone.'

7

As he went out, MacAdam almost collided with PC Scott in the doorway. He left with instructions that all except Janice and Noel, himself, and the remainder of the suspects, might now go to bed or otherwise disperse in whatever manner they pleased.

'*Get ivy and hull, woman,*' Fen sang as the door closed behind him, '*deck up thine house, and take this same brawn for to seethe and to souse.* I like the peremptory, patriarchal air of that carol,' he commented.

'Well, Scott, what results?' Wyndham asked.

'A blank, sir,' said the constable, swelling visibly with the consciousness of duty well performed. 'A complete blank. None of the guests knew or had heard of any of these persons' – he tapped the paper with the nail of his forefinger – 'prior to August, 1939.'

'Which is unhelpful,' Fen remarked. 'Well, never mind.'

'What exactly was the point of the question, sir?' Wyndham demanded.

'It concerns the Forrest case. Hadow will be able to tell you more about it than I can, but I suggest that we leave him until last.'

The clock on the mantelpiece struck one.

'Well, sir,' said Wyndham, eyeing it sleepily, 'who do you think we should see now?'

'It hardly matters, really. What about this priest – Nathan?'

'Very good, sir. Scott, ask Mr Nathan to step in here for

a minute. By the way,' Wyndham added when the constable was gone, 'isn't it odd that none of these guests should have *heard* of Hadow – he being a writer – before 1939?'

'He didn't start publishing until the war,' Fen explained absently; he seemed to be thinking of something else. 'Have you made any attempt to trace these gloves?'

'Not yet, sir. There hasn't been time.'

'Well, I suggest you show them to each of these people we interview. As they were left by the body, they're not likely to lead us anywhere. But we can try.'

In fact, the gloves proved to be Nathan's. He identified them without hesitation. He had left them, he said, in the pocket of his coat, and presumably anyone could have removed them. Obviously (he added rather uncertainly), if he had committed this appalling crime, he would not have used his own gloves; though on the other hand (here he grew noticeably depressed), he might have done, on the assumption that the police would suspect him the less for leaving so obvious a clue. It depended on the degree of sophistication one postulated in the criminal.

He had a light, quick, tenor voice, with a tendency to gabble; and Noel's description of him – 'High church, arty, blue in the jowl' – had certainly covered his most salient characteristics. In addition, he was noticeably thin – though broad-shouldered – and possessed remarkably penetrating brown eyes. His general appearance was untidy, and his coat was speckled with dandruff on the shoulders, collar and lapels.

'Jesus natus hodie,' Fen chanted. *'Nowell, nowell—'*

'Just a minute, please, sir,' Wyndham interrupted. This

persistent carolling was evidently fraying his nerves. 'Now, Mr Nathan, you were alone, I understand, during the game of hide-and-seek?'

Nathan was sitting forward in his chair, his bony hands clasped together on his knee.

'Yes, precisely,' he said. 'In point of fact I went to my own room. I'm sorry to say that on the whole I'm rather deficient in the party spirit. I was relieved when the gong was sounded five minutes earlier than had been anticipated.'

'Were you one of the earliest to return to the drawing room?'

'I don't think so. Nor, for that matter, one of the latest. Several people were crossing the hall as I came down the stairs.'

'I see. Did you know Mrs Munro well?'

'Hardly at all. I met her for the first time when I arrived the day before yesterday. To me she was just one of a number of hardly differentiated "other guests".'

'And after you returned to the drawing room?'

'I remained there until the crime was discovered. I think that quite a number of people can testify to my presence.'

In the hall outside, there was a low murmur of conversation as people went up to bed, and once they heard the front door open and shut, to allow the departure of an elderly couple who felt unable to stay in the house after what had happened. They apologised at length to MacAdam, who responded with suitable comprehension and penitence.

'And can you throw any light at all, sir,' said Wyndham, 'on either the attack on Miss Davenant or the murder of Mrs Munro?'

'As regards the former, no. I was unpacking in my room when it occurred. As regards the latter——' Nathan hesitated.

'Well, sir?'

Nathan gave the inspector a quick and rather chilly smile. 'A small point, and probably it means nothing. As I returned to the drawing room after the game, I saw someone emerge from the vestibule which leads into the long gallery.'

'Oh?' said Wyndham quickly. 'And who was that, sir?'

'His name is Simon Moore.'

8

Moore replaced Nathan, who returned to the others. He was scrupulously dressed, but offered a faint, unanalysable impression of shabbiness. There was a sort of generalised weariness about him, too: the weariness of a man who has spent his life striving for something which in his inmost heart he knows is not worthwhile – and has even then failed to obtain it.

He might have been forty years of age, with a tendency to plumpness and the dispiriting, automatic smile of the professional *bon homme* perpetually lingering on his lips. His black hair was remarkably thick and fine, and he wore rimless octagonal spectacles, which gave him a slightly transatlantic appearance. His manner throughout the interview, though superficially straightforward and agreeable, struck both Fen and Wyndham as being taut and strained. And there might be some justification for this, since his position had, obviously, its dangers.

He made no attempt to deny Nathan's assertion.

'Yes, I was in the vestibule,' he agreed in a soft, low-pitched voice. 'It's quite a comfortable little room, and I knew as well as anyone else did that the game wasn't going to be taken very seriously.'

'Did you enter the long gallery at all, sir?'

'No. Not at any time.'

'Did you see anyone else do so?'

'Yes,' said Moore unexpectedly. 'That's to say I didn't see them – it was pitch dark. But, I heard them.'

'Them?'

'Him, then,' said Moore with a touch of impatience. 'Or her – I don't know which. It was only one person, anyway. I'd just finished groping about for a chair when this person came in from the hall. For some reason or other I sat quite still and said nothing – I think I imagined that after all Duncan *was* going about looking for people. At all events, I don't think that whoever it was can have known that I was there. I noticed' – he paused for a moment – 'I noticed that he or she was breathing rather quickly and loudly, as though excited. But in the circumstances, that didn't surprise me much.'

'And you heard no one else go through into the long gallery?'

'No.'

'You're sure you can't say whether it was a man or a woman, sir? You see what I'm getting at, I've no doubt. Both Mrs Munro *and* someone else were in that gallery during the game of hide-and-seek.'

'Yes, I understand, but I can't help you. It was perfectly possible for anyone to enter the long gallery *before* I went into the vestibule. After the lights had gone out, I stayed put in the hall until most of the people had cleared off.'

'I see. Now, sir, did you hear any sounds from the long gallery while you were in the vestibule?'

'I heard sounds from all over the house,' Moore answered drily. 'Bumps and shrieks and giggles and whispers. You can't let a gang of people loose in the darkness, in a house which most of them don't properly know, without that happening. Mostly it was in the early stages, though, before everyone got settled. Where it all came from, I honestly can't say. One's sense of direction seems to go to pot in the darkness.'

'You mentioned whispers. If you heard whispering, it must surely have come from nearby?'

Moore took off his glasses to polish them. His weak sight made him look oddly defenceless.

'I suppose so,' he said, 'but it might equally well have come from the hall as from the long gallery. Of course, I couldn't distinguish any words.'

'And when the gong was sounded—'

'I went out almost immediately. In fact, I was one of the first to get to the drawing room. After that, I stayed there until – until I heard the news.'

'I'm afraid this is a personal question, but it must be asked. Were you in love with Mrs Munro?'

'No.' Moore flushed. 'But no doubt you've heard that I wanted to marry her.'

'Ah.' Wyndham evaded the slightly aggressive invitation to probe Moore's motives in the matter. 'You had asked her to marry you?'

'Yes. I asked her yesterday – that is, on the twenty-fourth. She refused.'

'I'm sorry,' said Wyndham with a bizarre and palpably insincere sympathy. 'Were you upset by her refusal?'

'Hardly. I intended to ask her again as soon as the opportunity offered.'

'Can you tell us *why* she refused you, sir?'

'She suggested that I only wanted to marry her for her money,' Moore replied coolly. 'That was her ostensible reason. Actually, of course, she was a minx. She got a great deal of fun out of having men tagging after her.'

'Was she particularly attached to anyone other than yourself?'

'She wasn't particularly attached to *me*, I can assure you … Anyway, the answer is no. She was prepared to allow almost any man to make love to her – up to a point – but apart from myself she had no regular devotees.' Moore paused, and as Wyndham said nothing, went on: 'I'm sorry to say that I didn't think her a very agreeable woman. She was what I should call a chaste wanton – suggestive of positively Turkish carnalities, but in practice as forbidding as a block of ice.'

Wyndham appeared to be considering the possible characteristics of Turkish carnality.

'As far as I knew,' Moore concluded, 'there was only one person to whom she was wholeheartedly and unselfishly devoted – her brother. And it seems that he's in prison.'

'Ah,' said Fen significantly. For some time he had been maintaining a gruesome and unnatural silence. 'You interest me enormously.'

When Moore had gone, and PC Scott had been dispatched to fetch Richard Neame, he drank some whisky and added: 'I suppose the point of your last questions was to discover if

Louise Munro was likely to have made an assignation with anyone in the long gallery. Evidently it wasn't only likely, but virtually certain. Everyone seems to agree that she was as promiscuous as a rabbit.'

'As a rabbit,' Wyndham repeated, nodding mournfully. 'Though as to Turkish carnalities, I should have said rabbits were rather addicted to *them*.'

Richard Neame appeared promptly. He was a stolid man of thirty to thirty-five with a defensive air which Fen concluded was due less to present circumstances than to his avocation. Most schoolmasters acquire it, in one form or another; it is almost a necessity in dealing with the ghastly perspicuity of the young. With it went an authoritativeness which was vaguely offensive. It was evident, moreover, that he was far more concerned with the potential fate of Patricia Davenant than with the actual immolation of Louise Munro – regarding which, indeed, he displayed considerable indifference.

He announced, rather surprisingly, that during the game of hide-and-seek he had locked himself in a lavatory. He had wished, he explained stiffly, to be with Miss Davenant, but a slight disagreement earlier in the evening had made that undesirable. He had found the game trying, and thought it on the whole unnecessary. When it was over, he had returned immediately to the drawing room.

'And what impelled you, sir, to join in the search for Mrs Munro?'

Neame appeared taken aback. He stammered a little. 'I simply – I simply felt that it was my duty to assist.'

'Quite so. And will you tell us what Mrs Munro said before she died?'

'All I heard was that Patricia was in danger.' Neame had lost some of his stiffness and spoke more vigorously. 'That was enough for me. If you'd seen the ghastly state that wretched woman was in ...' His self-consciousness abruptly returned. 'Naturally, I left, and made straight for Patricia's – Miss Davenant's – room. Simon Moore went with me. She'd just finished changing when we arrived and, thank God, she was all right. We looked about the room a bit, and at last it occurred to me to make sure that her medicines and so forth were all right. I put a little of the tonic in my mouth, and asked her what it normally tasted like ...' He gestured angrily. 'The rest you know.'

'Exactly, sir,' Wyndham's tones were soothing. 'And you can throw no light on the previous attack on Miss Davenant?'

'I wish I could. I should like to get my hands on whoever was responsible.'

Fen regarded him thoughtfully. He had heard sufficient of Neame's infatuation with Patricia Davenant to make him suspicious of its sincerity. But that the man *was* infatuated he had now not the smallest doubt.

'Had you known Mrs Munro long?' he asked.

'Didn't meet her till I came here,' said Neame shortly. The subject of Louise Munro seemed almost to irritate him. And apparently he had some suspicion that heartlessness might be imputed to him, for he mumbled conventionally: 'Very tragic affair.'

He departed uttering various admonitions about the future safety of Patricia Davenant, the responsibility for which, he stated, rested entirely on the police.

'*He* didn't try to kill her, anyway,' said Fen after the door had closed behind him. '*Although at Yule it bloweth cool,*' he burst out suddenly, '*and frost doth grip the fingers …*'

He was cut short by the arrival of Sergeant Stokes, in a state of high excitement.

'I've been through Mrs Munro's room,' the sergeant announced, 'and made two discoveries that I think'll prove to be important.' He beamed expectantly at his superior.

'Well, don't stand there,' said Wyndham, justifiably annoyed, 'with that oafish smirk on your face. What have you found?'

'First of all,' said the Sergeant dramatically, 'a letter which shows that Mrs Munro was blackmailing someone.' He handed Wyndham a plain white envelope with the flap tucked in. 'And second, what I'm pretty certain is Miss Davenant's diary.'

9

A stasis occurred while the provenance of the diary was checked and Patricia Davenant's fingerprints were taken. In the end it proved that the only prints on the diary were those of Patricia herself and of Louise Munro.

'So Mrs Munro took it,' said Wyndham blankly. 'And I suppose it was she who attacked Miss Davenant. But in God's name, why …?'

He flicked over the pages of the little green-bound book. 'Surely there's nothing in this she could possibly want to see. It's little more than a list of engagements, and as far as I can see, there's no one in this party, barring Neame and MacAdam, who's as much as mentioned in it. And there's not a single damaging secret that I can make out. What do you think about it, sir?'

'I think,' said Fen from the depths of his armchair, 'that Louise Munro was as disappointed as you are; that she was expecting damaging secrets, too, and likewise failed to find them.'

'Is it possible that she was responsible for the strychnine?'

'And had a fit of death-bed repentance? It's possible,' Fen admitted grudgingly, 'but on the whole I don't think so. That would leave Louise Munro's murder out of account, and I'm certain these things are all bound up together. Believe me, there's only *one* murderer running around loose – and just as well, too,' he ended somewhat peevishly, 'or we should all be in our graves in a winking.'

'Well, now, sir – this letter.' Wyndham unfolded it to read it again. It was typewritten on a plain sheet of white paper, and ran: '*I am tired of blackmail. You may expect a visit from me soon.*' Wyndham flicked the edge of the paper with his forefinger. 'It would seem as though Louise Munro's blackmail victim had got sick of whatever extortions were going on and decided to put a stop to them once and for all. That sort of thing's been done often enough before.'

'It seems so,' Fen agreed, 'though I think there's an alternative explanation ... The letter was found in that plain envelope?'

'Yes. *Apparently* it wasn't posted.'

'Ah,' Fen murmured absently. 'I rather think it must have been put in Louise Munro's room the evening everyone arrived – probably a short time before the diary was stolen ... Yes ...'

He fell silent. Wyndham saw that he was concentrating

on some problem or other, and respected his absorption. But when Fen spoke again, it was only to say:

'What orders have you given Scott about this gang of suspects in the drawing room?'

'Orders?'

'I mean, are you allowing them to move about the house at their own sweet will?'

'Lord, no. They've been in the drawing room ever since we arrived, and there they stay until we've finished with them.'

'Of course, the evidence may have vanished before you got here,' Fen murmured obscurely. 'In that case, I'm not sure that an arrest would be justified ... MacAdam's the man to ask ...' He shook himself irritably out of his daydream. 'Anyway, Inspector, that precaution may save our bacon ... Shall we see Patricia Davenant now?'

10

The clock struck a quarter to two as Patricia Davenant came in, but despite the lateness of the hour she looked fresh and untired. She was wearing a plain brown coat and skirt which set off the magnificent lines of her figure, and Fen observed that her make-up was so well applied as to suggest a professional interest in the matter. Unquestionably she was beautiful; but the chief impression one received was of an unthinking tranquillity, combined with a sort of naivety such as one often sees in actresses, ballet dancers and other women whose job it is to display themselves publicly. She sat down, crossed her legs, and looked expectantly and unselfconsciously at the two men.

'What is your occupation, Miss Davenant?' Wyndham asked.

'I'm a model,' she replied directly. 'You know – magazine covers, advertisements, and so on.'

'Your age?'

'Twenty-five.'

'And you're engaged to be married to Mr Neame?'

She glanced at the diamond ring on the fourth finger of her left hand. 'Yes. I've only known him a few months, but I'm very, very fond of him.'

'You had a quarrel earlier this evening?'

'We've made it up now. It was nothing.'

'Still, it was enough to make you refuse to go with him during the game of hide-and-seek.'

Patricia regarded the inspector wonderingly. 'I thought if I was stand-offish it would do him good,' she said; and added ingenuously: 'Some men who've made love to me say I'm not enough of a *coquette*.'

'Where did you go, during the game?'

'I? I hid in the cloakroom. You know – by the front door. I thought as it was near the starting place Duncan wouldn't be likely to look there.'

'Didn't you understand that – well, that the game was more or less an excuse to enable' – Wyndham reddened, and becoming annoyed at this, reddened still more – 'to enable people to get away together?' he concluded obliquely.

'Was it? I didn't realise.'

(And as a matter of fact, Fen reflected, it wouldn't occur to this girl that any excuse was needed for leaving a party in order to make love.)

Wyndham returned to the attack. 'I gather some accident happened to your dress?' he said.

'Oh, such a damned nuisance,' Patricia answered petulantly. 'In the darkness I got caught up on a hook or something, and my shoulder strap broke. It wasn't a man or anything,' she added rather vaguely.

'So when the game was over, you went upstairs to change?'

'Yes. That's why I'm wearing these things. I didn't bring another evening frock.'

'And then?'

'Well, the first I knew of anything being wrong was when Richard and Simon came panting in to say I was in danger. Even then it took me ages to get anything coherent out of Richard.'

'What happened after that?'

'Happened?' Patricia felt in her handbag, brought out a tiny cambric handkerchief, and pinched the end of her nose with it in that delicate parody of blowing which women affect. 'Nothing really happened. Richard flapped about for a minute or two until Duncan came up to tell us about Louise dying, and trying to give the name of the murderer and so on, and then Richard flapped about again, and by the time he'd discovered the stuff in the medicine the police had arrived and we were all marched down to the drawing room.'

'Do you know if you have any enemies, Miss Davenant?'

'I'm sure I haven't,' said Patricia. 'I think most people like me ... Oh, well, I suppose *someone* doesn't, if my tonic really *was* poisoned, but I can't think who it could be.' She hesitated. 'Who was it stole my diary?'

'We think it was Mrs Munro.'

'Louise?' Patricia was almost indignant. 'But how *silly*: why should anyone want to steal it at all?'

'We were hoping you could help us over that.'

'Well, there's absolutely nothing in it. It's really only an engagement book.'

'Nothing that could – ah – compromise you?'

'Of course not.' Obviously Patricia did not in the least resent this question, but her blue eyes were wide with astonishment.

'Had you known Mrs Munro for long?'

'No, I only met her two days ago. I remember she arrived almost at the same moment as Richard and me, and Duncan introduced us in the hall.'

'You came here with Mr Neame?'

'Yes, we stayed together in a hotel in Thame last night. In separate rooms, of course,' Patricia explained gravely. 'Richard's very particular about that sort of thing.'

Wyndham, mindful of the traditions of the Force, suppressed a grin.

'But I still can't see why Louise should steal my diary,' said Patricia, sincerely puzzled. 'I liked her, though of course she was terribly nervy.'

Fen asked a question. 'I believe your typewriter was used at the same time the diary was stolen?'

'Yes. Anyway, I found it open on the desk in my room.' Patricia frowned earnestly. 'Of course that *might* have been done *before* the diary was taken. I was one of the first to arrive, you see, and didn't bother to unpack much, and changed very quickly downstairs. And then later I found I'd forgotten a handkerchief, and went back, and it all happened. But anyway, it isn't my typewriter.'

Fen displayed interest. 'Whose is it, then?'

'I borrowed it about a month ago,' said Patricia. 'Someone told me I ought to write a book about my experiences, but I found I couldn't manage it. So I brought the typewriter here to give back. It belongs to Peter Hadow.'

11

'Well, Hadow is the last,' said Wyndham with a sigh of relief, when Patricia had been sent back to the drawing room.

'And in some ways the most important, I suspect,' Fen rejoined thoughtfully. 'If I'm not much mistaken, he'll supply us with the motive – which at present is the most obscure feature of the whole affair.'

The novelist arrived yawning prodigiously. He had driven up that day from Torquay, he explained, and although some form of revelry might have kept him awake until this late hour, the effort of sitting about in the drawing room had been almost too much for him. Wyndham apologised for this in his own dulcet way, and introduced Hadow to Fen. They settled down to the consumption of MacAdam's whisky, an oddly contrasted trio: Wyndham's bulky form fitting immovable into his chair, Fen tall, lanky and restless, and Hadow sprawled back, his dark hair tousled, his pince-nez clutched in his right hand, his mouth opening and shutting regularly, and his small, weak blue eyes drowsy and inattentive.

'Let me answer your questions before you ask them,' he said mildly. 'My name is Peter Hadow, my age thirty-four, my occupation the writing of detective novels. I arrived at this house about 10.37 this evening to find it as black and ghastly as the tomb, and was met at the front door by Duncan MacAdam, bearing a naked and tremulous light. While I was trying to discover the reason for all this, he ordered an aged man, whom I at first took to be the butler, to beat upon a gong, and when this unaccountable rite was over, went and switched on some lights. I was divested of my hat and coat, and taken into the drawing room for a drink. People began to appear in numbers. I saw one whom I knew – namely Patricia Davenant – and was introduced to her betrothed, Richard Neame, with whom I've just been carrying on a turgid dialogue regarding the Sociological Significance of the Detective Novel. Of course detective novels have no more sociological significance than any other kind of novel, but he's not the sort of person who could ever be made to realise that. Poor dear, he has some fancy about the detective novel being connected with the rise of Nazism.'

Hadow paused to grin at Wyndham, who was eyeing him warily. It was apparent that Hadow was by no means entirely sober.

'Forgive the pseudo-literary chatter,' he went on. 'For some reason whisky always has this effect on me. *Le style, c'est l'alcool* ... Where was I? Ah, yes.

'In addition to Richard Neame, I was introduced to an exceedingly pretty and forward wench named Janice, and to her predestined victim, a canny but nonetheless fated young man who tells me he's interested in Assyriology, though I hardly know whether to believe that. At about 10.45 or 10.50 Duncan took me up to my room and left me there, so that

I'm not accounted for until I went downstairs ten minutes or so later. As a matter of fact I washed my hands and felt the bed and made a feeble attempt to unpack and peered into the wardrobe and did all the other things one does on arriving in a strange house … Anyway, I eventually returned downstairs – as I said. And the next thing was that just as I'd thought up an admirable word for a charade, we were all in the thick of it, with the girl I came here to meet desperately dead.'

Wyndham, who had been surveying the point of his pencil during this monologue, looked up. 'You came here to meet Mrs Munro?'

'I think of her as Louise Benest,' said Hadow a trifle inconsequently. 'Yes. I wanted to talk to her.' He glanced at Fen. 'You remember the Forrest case, just before the war?'

'The outlines,' Fen replied slowly. 'It was put rather out of one's head by the invasion of Poland. Would you mind running over it for our benefit? I gather you're more or less an expert on the subject.'

Hadow by now was observably less somnolent. 'It did take my fancy,' he admitted, 'to the extent that I decided to write a novel round it. Of course it wasn't for the sake of the novel that I went into the details of the affair. Crime as actually practised has little or nothing to do with the detective novel, which is a conventional-unreal *genre*, as purely imaginative as an interplanetary tale or a mediaeval cosmology. Naturally it has to be concerned with what's *possible*, but what's *probable* is practically outside its sphere …' Hadow stopped abruptly. 'What was I talking about?' he demanded.

'The Forrest case,' Wyndham reminded him severely.

'Oh, yes. Well, the thing got to interest me for its own sake, and I went on delving into it long after my book was finished.' Hadow paused to light a cigarette. 'It had one or two curious features, you see: the third man, and the missing dagger …

'You know it all occurred in Shrewsbury. I went there during the second year of the war, put up at the "Lion", and had a good look round. It's a pleasant town, not too large, with the Severn running round it in a kind of horseshoe; at the centre of the horseshoe is the toll bridge leading over to Kingsland and the Schools.

'The actual scene of the crime was the office of a solicitor in Pride Hill, which is, I suppose, the main shopping street. The office is a flat, really, about halfway down on the English Bridge side. You get to it by a flight of uncarpeted stairs leading up from an alleyway. The window of the main office overlooks a courtyard at the back, also reached from the alleyway. There's your setting. It hasn't any importance in itself; what happened there might just as well have happened at a dozen other places in the town.

'The protagonists are a nightwatchman called Webb; PC Knight, of the Shropshire Constabulary; Edward Forrest; Louise Benest; her brother Charles; and a man who may or may not have been Andrew, Edward Forrest's brother.'

Hadow relit his cigarette, which had gone out. 'I don't know if all this is too detailed for you?' he enquired.

'No,' said Fen briefly. His manner was intent. 'Go on.'

'Louise and Charles Benest were living together at that time, in a house up on Kingsland. They had enough money of their own to avoid doing anything, and Charles had not, for medical reasons, been called up. He was about twenty-five, straightforward, ordinary, moderately intelligent; and he was devoted to his sister, as she was to him. Louise – Louise Munro to you – seems to have been a more unstable character than her brother, prone to fits of depression, and with another definite psychological kink which I'll tell you about in a moment. Of course at that time she wasn't very much more than a schoolgirl. Both the parents, by the way, were dead.

'In the last week of August, 1939, Edward Forrest arrived to stay with them for a week or two. Charles had met him at Oxford, and had apparently been fascinated by him to the extent of wholly overlooking the fact that Forrest had a basically childish mind – though superficially he was worldly, witty in a sixth-formish kind of way, and charming. Probably his motive in accepting the invitation had to do with Louise, but one doesn't know about that – nor does it matter much, now that he's occupying a plot of earth in a prison cemetery.

'He had only one relation, a brother who had been living for some years abroad. Note that word "abroad". Nothing more definite ever emerged on the subject. Moreover – and this is the important point – it's tolerably certain that the brother had changed his name and become a national of some other country. Ten years previously he had become involved in some trivial swindle, and had somehow contrived to leave England – after which no trace of him was ever found. That may sound fantastic, but there are two points to be borne in mind: (a) that he had not had a photograph taken since he was a child; and (b) that although in that Utopia to which we're all so eagerly looking forward everyone's movements will doubtless be recorded from font to coffin, there were plenty of loopholes in those days.'

Hadow was absorbed in his narrative; all signs of tiredness had vanished.

'You see what I'm getting at,' he continued. 'The extraordinary *shadowiness* of this figure. Even his age remains uncertain. Unless he's changed very much, there are presumably still people in this country – landladies and so on – who could identify him, but after the lapse of years it would be a shaky business. One imagines that he himself was of that opinion otherwise he'd scarcely have returned.

'Edward Forrest referred to his brother, when he spoke of him to Charles and Louise Benest, as "Andrew", and that seems to have been his right name. The parents – poor folk – died quite early, and Andrew was left to look after his younger brother Edward. He worked, and scraped, and saved (obviously he was devoted to Edward), and he can't have been entirely without ability, because he managed to get together enough money to send Edward to Oxford, whereafter Edward got himself a job and became tolerably affluent. But in the meantime, Andrew had tried to hasten the process by the swindle aforesaid, and so vanished from the scene – until, perhaps, that evening of August, 1939.

'I'm sorry to take so long in getting to the actual crime, but after the trial of Edward Forrest, the presence of Andrew in England began to make itself felt; and for that reason it's important to understand how he came to be so exceedingly elusive. One thing is certain, I think – namely that Andrew didn't return to England with a passport. If you have some kind of boat, it's not at all difficult to get unobserved into any maritime country in the world. Two days after the affair in Shrewsbury, a small motor launch was found abandoned in a cove near Brixham. Perhaps that was what he used – who knows?

'Naturally, all these facts about Andrew weren't known to Louise and Charles Benest – or at least not until the time of the trial, and then only partially. Andrew Forrest was a somewhat remote and improbable figure, and counsel didn't have much to say about him. Edward merely told the Benests that his brother was arriving by the late train on August 17, 1939. Evidently they had kept in touch.'

Hadow paused. 'Well, it's pretty certain that he did arrive. A taxi-man remembers driving someone to the house on Kingsland. But it seems that the nearest he got to his brother was to hear the shot with which Edward Forrest murdered Webb the nightwatchman in the office on Pride Hill.'

12

'That evening – August 17, 1939 – Charles Benest, Louise Benest and Edward Forrest got drunk together. Or perhaps it would be more correct to say that only Edward Forrest got seriously drunk. They did a round of the pubs and then returned to the house and went on drinking there. And they argued about crime.

'The discussion followed one of its familiar courses. It ended with Forrest's maintaining that to commit a success-ful crime, and get away with it, was the easiest thing in the world; and he offered to prove it, there and then, by commit-ting a robbery.

'It's obvious that the others tried to dissuade him, but people when drunk are not easily dissuaded, and probably they felt obliged to go with him (since he persisted), in the hope of stopping him when it came to the point. As you'll hear, they didn't succeed.

'The victim Edward Forrest selected was a solicitor with whom Charles and Louise had had dealings in some matter of property dealings which were unsatisfactory to them. They had mentioned his name to Edward Forrest earlier on the same day, and now nothing would satisfy him but that this unfortunate man's office should be the scene of the experiment; the drunk often develop an exaggerated sense of retribution.

'The walk from Kingsland to Pride Hill takes about a quarter of an hour, and it must have sobered Forrest to some extent – though not enough, unfortunately, to divert him from his purpose. He had left a hastily scribbled note for Andrew, indicating where they had gone, and why; and presumably Andrew's taxi passed them soon after they had set out.

'Well, they got to the office. It was one o'clock in the morning of the 18th. The streets were deserted and the street lamps out, but there was a half-moon which gave them sufficient light to be able to see what they were doing. One needn't expand this part of the story unduly. It's quite easy to imagine the efforts which the Benests made to stop Forrest's idiot scheme. The door in the alleyway, which gave on the stairs leading up to the flat, had a Yale lock; but it also had a glass panel at the top, and by breaking this Forrest was able to get in. The other two followed him up to the outer office;

there they made a last attempt to prevent the whole silly business. But Forrest would have none of it; it wasn't a crime, he said; whatever he took, he'd return next morning by post; he merely intended to show that the thing could be done.

'So they left him there.

'Even so, they didn't go right away; it would have been better for them if they had. They lingered down below, and Louise went round to the courtyard at the back. There she saw the light go on in the main office, and Forrest drunkenly rummaging through the drawers of the desk. The fates had chosen to leave a loaded revolver in one of them. Louise deposed at the trial that he examined it carefully, opening and closing the chambers several times.

'The first outsider to arrive at the scene was Webb. It was his job to keep an eye on a whole block of houses up that side of Pride Hill, and he had heard the noise of breaking glass. One doesn't know whether he saw either of the Benests. Anyway, he went straight up the stairs to the office, and there Forrest was foolish enough to try and hold him up with his revolver.

'Louise saw the whole thing happen, and it was over very quickly. Webb realised at once that he had a drunk to deal with, and moved forward a step or two to reason with him; at which Forrest deliberately shot the man in the stomach. He died very quickly from internal haemorrhage.

'We come now to PC Knight, patrolling Pride Hill from the Kingsland direction, and with a belated wayfarer hurrying up behind him. It's one hypothesis, of course, that this wayfarer was brother Andrew. Knight caught only a glimpse of him, and that totally insufficient for identification purposes. The weak moonlight was to blame, and the sudden report of the pistol, which distracted Knight's attention. For a moment both men stopped dead. Then the constable ran forward to the alleyway. What became of brother Andrew – if it was brother Andrew – no one knows; he wasn't seen again, and presumably he cleared off as quickly as possible. In his position he could hardly wish to get mixed up with anything involving the police – whatever his affection for Edward.

'Knight, as I've said, ran for the alleyway, and entered the door at the bottom of the staircase leading to the office. But before he could get further someone overtook him and struck at him from behind with a knife. The wounds in themselves were not serious, but Knight overbalanced and struck his head on the handrail. He was unconscious for two minutes or so. Edward Forrest, panic-stricken, performed the insane action of flinging down the revolver (with his fingerprints all over it), and then fled; and Charles and Louise went back to Kingsland. But there had been sufficient noise to raise an alarm; the police were interviewing Charles and Louise half an hour later; and Edward Forrest was arrested next morning in Bristol.'

Hadow paused, lit a fresh cigarette, and swallowed his whisky at a gulp.

'Charles and Louise,' he resumed, 'being tolerably sensible people, made a clean breast of the whole affair, and Charles admitted to the attack on Knight; he had done it, he said, on a momentary impulse which he now recognised to have been insane, in the hope of keeping Louise out of the affair; and to anyone acquainted with the mutual affection of brother and sister, this seemed a perfectly plausible explanation. The weapon, it appeared, was a sharpish dagger of Indian design which was used in the outer office as a paper knife. Charles said that he had picked it up with some vague idea of intimidating Edward Forrest, and had kept it in his hand when he left the flat; he added, moreover, that he had flung it down immediately after using it. But when the police looked for it, it had gone, and no trace of it has ever been found from that day to this.

'In parenthesis, I had a notion at one time that it might have been *Andrew* who attacked Knight, in the hope of getting his brother Edward out of the mess. But it soon became obvious that that theory wasn't tenable. For one thing, there was no earthly reason why Charles Benest should protect Andrew to get access to the dagger in time – and it certainly looks as though that was the weapon used, since it disappeared so completely. I only mention the fallacies in this notion of mine in case the same idea has occurred to you.

'Forrest came up for trial at the Shrewsbury Assizes in the autumn of 1939. In those days, if you remember, we were all in hourly expectation of annihilating German air raids, so the case wasn't much noticed in the press. But I was already interested in some features of the case, and I managed to attend the trial.

'It lasted only a couple of days, and from the first the issue was in considerable doubt. There was no question, of course, as to whether Edward Forrest had actually shot Webb or not – the fingerprints on the gun disposed finally and effectively of that problem; but the defence maintained that the thing had been wholly an accident, and in addition that Forrest's drunkenness was evidence that no guilty state of mind existed. So the crux of the trial was Louise's assertion, which the defence wasn't able to shake, that Forrest had carefully examined the revolver on first discovering it. He, of course, denied this, and the trial really boiled down to his word against hers – in fact, to a matter of personalities, and the impression they made on the jury. Louise won hands down. The war had got people into a state of moral fervour, and the sheer inexcusable wantonness of Forrest's actions that night told heavily against him. He was brought in guilty and condemned to death.

'There were appeals for mitigation of sentence. They failed. Edward Forrest was hanged in January, 1940, and to all intents and purposes it was Louise Benest who hanged him.

'In some ways, Charles Benest was almost as unlucky as Forrest. His case came up later in the same Assizes, and of course under the same judge. There had been some question of indicting both him and Louise as principals in the second degree in the murder of Webb, but that was dropped, and Charles was charged with causing grievous bodily harm to prevent an arrest. In view of the fact that he pleaded guilty, there was considerable astonishment when he got the maximum sentence of fourteen years. That means that up to now he's done about half of it. Louise, of course, escaped altogether.'

Hadow smiled, a little grimly. 'We're coming now to the crux of the matter, in so far as it concerns what's been happening here. You'll guess that it has to do with brother Andrew. Evidently he regarded Louise as solely responsible for Edward's hanging, and in a sense he was quite right. On the day the execution was carried out, Louise was attacked in her own drawing room, and an attempt made to strangle her. She didn't see the attacker, and the arrival of a servant drove him away before he could finish the job. There was no doubt that it was brother Andrew – she had had typewritten letters accusing her not only of his death, but also of instigating the crime for which he was condemned. Brother Andrew's affection for Edward had driven him a little crazy, you see; he wanted vengeance. Perhaps slashing a woman's bare back with a sharp knife would have satisfied him ...

'Louise took the letters to the police, and asked for protection – which she got. No more letters arrived, and there was no further untoward incident. She married Munro, a rich man, and shortly afterwards he was killed in a flying accident. Apparently brother Andrew had vanished into limbo – until, that is to say' – with an expressive gesture – 'tonight.'

Hadow stopped to refill his glass, and looked at them quizzically.

'Well, it's been a long story,' he said. 'But it seems to me that if you're looking for a motive, there it is, ready-made. Your problem now is to find out who, or what, is Andrew Forrest; and to that there just isn't any clue. He might be MacAdam, or Neame, or Nathan, or Moore—'

'Or, of course, yourself,' said Fen in an oddly colourless voice.

Wyndham stirred himself. 'There's one more thing, sir. You mentioned that Louise Benest – or Louise Munro, as I prefer to call her – had some kind of psychological kink. What was that?'

'Oh, yes, I forgot.' Hadow smiled. 'She suffered from genuine, bona fide, certifiable claustrophobia ... What do you make of that?'

13

Hadow was conducted back to the drawing room by PC Scott.

'*Heap on more wood, the wind is chill,*' Fen carolled gently. '*But let it whistle as it will, we'll keep our Christmas merry still* ... Well, Inspector?'

'Well, sir: is that our motive?'

Fen nodded. 'I think so. Oh yes, I think so.'

'I've got to agree. But I scarcely see how the attempt to kill Miss Davenant comes into it – unless in some way she knows who the murderer is.'

'Very unlikely,' said Fen, and added provokingly: 'It's all perfectly natural, Inspector. It all fits.'

'It doesn't fit to me,' said Wyndham staunchly. 'I suppose now we shall have to go delving into the past history of all these five men ... By the way, would Hadow have given us such a generous resumé of the case if he'd been Andrew Forrest?'

'We were bound to find out pretty soon about Louise Munro's connection with the Forrest case – in fact, as soon as I heard her maiden name I remembered the gist of the business. Besides, it was known that Hadow had come here specifically to talk to Louise Munro about it. That being so, he couldn't very well pretend ignorance.'

'Was his account correct?'

'Oh, yes, I think so.'

'But anyway' – Wyndham reverted to the previous subject – 'I don't see how I can hold *all* of those five on suspicion while we rummage into their pasts.' He stared blankly before him for a moment, and then said: 'Lord, sir, I'm stuck. Advise me what to do.'

'Just detain the one who's guilty. You've got plenty of evidence for that. Once you have him in your hands, you've got plenty of time to get him identified, trace his movements, and so forth.'

Wyndham sighed. 'If one only knew which …'

'Oh, I know,' said Gervase Fen blandly. 'I was tolerably certain after that first interview with Noel and Janice, and everything since then has gone to confirm my suspicions.'

Wyndham stared at him. 'You're joking, sir.'

'No, I'm not,' said Fen testily. 'I'm incapable of jokes at three o'clock in the morning.'

'Who do you mean, then?'

Fen told him.

'Well, I'm damned,' Wyndham commented unemotionally. 'I shouldn't have imagined … But why do you think so?'

Fen made certain explanations. 'Of course,' he concluded, 'it's *slightly* psychological. But still …'

'Psychological my foot!' Wyndham exclaimed vehemently. 'It's plain, simple and obvious, and I can't think how I was so stupid as not to see it. Oh, we'll have that gentleman locked up in less than no time.'

'I think we might try Patricia Davenant's typewriter first,' Fen suggested. 'Also, there's a question I want to ask MacAdam … Let's get it all over and done with, and then we can go home. Have you got the letter? Good.'

They left the study and crossed the hall to the drawing room. A dispirited little group was sitting round the fire.

'Hello,' said Fen. 'You all look very wan … MacAdam, do you let people know, when you invite them to your parties, what other guests are going to be there?'

MacAdam stood up to answer. His plump face was drawn and tired, and his hair more dishevelled than ever. 'Yes, always,' he said shortly. 'Any objections?'

'None,' said Fen mildly.

MacAdam was very near anger. 'Inspector,' he snapped, 'is it really necessary for us to sit here all night?'

'In just five minutes, sir,' said Wyndham mildly, 'you'll all be able to go to bed. I shall be back shortly … By the way, where are Mr Carter and Miss Mond?'

PC Scott came up, red in the face. 'I'm afraid I'm responsible, sir. I allowed them to go into the library. They were very persistent, and I thought …' He stammered himself into silence.

Wyndham glanced at Fen, who said: 'They may as well make love while they can enjoy it. Not that it's all that enjoyable, anyway,' he added gloomily. 'Let's go upstairs.'

Patricia Davenant's room was all white – curtains, carpets, and rugs. The bed, the wardrobe and the dressing table were of highly polished Indian rosewood, and the light came from frosted globes sunk in the ceiling. Patricia's clothes and belongings were scattered untidily about. A door on the right, which Fen investigated, led into a private bathroom. Fen pointed this out to Wyndham, who nodded.

'That would provide the opportunity,' he said. 'But to make sure we can ask about it.'

They found the typewriter, which was a portable one, and Fen screwed a piece of blank paper into it.

'How does it go?' he asked. 'Ah, yes ... *"I am tired of blackmail. You may expect a visit from me soon."*'

He tapped away inexpertly for some moments. 'Damn,' he said. 'I've hurt my finger on the shift lock.'

Wyndham compared the two sheets of paper. 'Yes,' he announced, 'I think the letter was obviously typed on this machine. You can see, for one thing, that the *m*'s out of alignment. But I'll get an expert to deal with it, for the purposes of the trial.'

Fen straightened himself, stretched, and yawned. 'So that's that,' he remarked. 'Oh, my dear paws, how sleepy I feel ... You'll search his belongings for the dagger, of course. And I should *think* there may be some prints taken from it, all duly and correctly attested – though of course a surface like that will keep prints for years, if it's not mucked about.'

'I'm very grateful to you, sir,' said Wyndham hesitatingly. 'If you hadn't pointed out that one simple thing to me, he might have been able to get clear of the country.'

'That's all right,' said Fen. 'Besides, I'm grateful to you, too. This business got me away from a children's party which descends on my house like a black cloud every Christmas Eve. And if there's one thing more horrible than violent death, it's the sight and sound of a large number of the young simultaneously enjoying themselves ... Well, I suppose you'd better collect your man.'

'It'll be a pleasure,' Wyndham murmured. 'From almost every point of view, it'll be a pleasure.'

14

Actually it was Janice who had persuaded PC Scott to let them go into the library. Noel was too tired to be anxious for anything but bed. There was a faint glow in the middle of the heap of white ashes in the fireplace, and Noel put a log on top of it; it burned feebly for about a minute, and then went out. They huddled over it seated together on a small sofa.

'There,' said Janice. 'This is better, isn't it?'

'You seem to have no sense of cold whatever,' Noel answered ungraciously. 'You're full of disgusting animal vitality.'

'Are you really interested in Assyriology? How funny. Tell me how the Assyrians made love.'

'They made love in exactly the same way that everybody else makes love. And the only thing I'm interested in at present is my health.'

'Shall I sit on your knee?'

'On the whole, no. I wonder when we're going to be able to get to bed.'

'Not until the parson has blessed us with bell and book, Noel.'

'I have a bad cold.'

'Don't be so fussy, darling. Have you ever been in love?'

'Never.'

'Not with Patricia?'

'Not with anyone.'

'You may kiss me if you wish.'

'I don't wish.'

'On the whole that's just as well,' said Janice judicially. 'Because you're not very competent at making love.'

'Oh really?' said Noel, nettled.

'For example, if you'd never met me until this moment, how would you begin making love to me?'

'No, Janice, I refuse to be caught that way.'

'I'm not trying to *catch* you, idiot. Tell me what you'd do, and I'll tell you whether it's good technique or not.'

'Well, I suppose I should say something like: "You're really very beautiful …"'

'Yes, that's just the point, you see.'

'What's just the point, in God's name?'

'It's purely imbecile to trot out all that mildewed stuff.'

'One must *say* something first. A sort of warning. Like the red flag they put out before guns are going to go off.'

'No. It's quite superfluous.'

'I can't help that. It's a habit.'

'Very well. Go on.'

'Then I should say something on the lines of: "Your eyes are an enchanting blue."'

'They're brown.'

'I wasn't talking about *your* eyes. I was talking about the eyes of some hypothetical woman I've never met before.'

'My mother's eyes are brown, too. It runs in the family. Something to do with heredity.'

'Heredity. There's that limerick about …'

'I know it. Will you put your arm round me?'

'If you insist. But it's very uncomfortable for the man.'

'It's very uncomfortable for the woman, too.'

'Why do you allow it, then?'

'*I* always thought men liked doing it. One must throw

them an occasional crumb. I think I'll sit on your knee after all,' said Janice, doing so. 'There. Isn't that nice?'

'It helps to keep me warm,' Noel admitted grudgingly.

'Darling, *why* don't you like me?'

'Janice, you're an intolerable little flirt. You should be spanked.'

'You may spank me if you like, but not too hard.'

'Don't you realise that no man has any use for a woman who runs after him?'

'Oh, no?' said Janice softly.

Noel took her up in his arms and deposited her firmly and not particularly gently in a chair.

'Understand this,' he said, 'once and for all: *I have not the slightest intention of marrying you or anyone else*. Now, is that perfectly clear?'

'Yes, Noel,' said Janice meekly.

15

After a week's honeymoon in Scotland, Noel and Janice returned south to act as witnesses at the trial for murder of Andrew Forrest. They stopped for a night in Oxford, putting up at the Mace and Sceptre, and after dinner went to see Fen at his rooms in St Christopher's. They found him biting a pencil and trying to write a detective novel; he was obviously relieved at having an excuse for neglecting it.

'Well, well,' he greeted them. 'All congratulations. I'm sorry I wasn't able to get to the wedding. Have you had a good honeymoon?'

'It's been very satisfactory, thank you,' said Janice demurely. Fen bustled about finding them drinks.

'You must tell us what's been happening,' said Noel, when they were at last settled. 'We've lost touch with everything.'

'His identity's been proved,' Fen answered. 'Which is most of the battle. And Crispin is proposing to write the case up. I suppose I shall have to get in touch with him about it – poor old chap, he gets terribly muddled …'

'I still don't understand how you *knew*,' said Janice.

'Ah,' said Fen complacently. 'Well, I shall now explain; and don't try to stop me, because it's a great and ancient tradition which must not be broken.

'Of course, the lynchpin of the whole case lay in the words which Louise Munro spoke just before she died. I've no doubt you remember them – *"Patricia … in danger … help her"*. And a little later: *"Mustn't be destroyed … I'll tell you … who …"*

'From the first, those words puzzled me, and I was careful to ask if you thought Louise was sane when she spoke them.

'MacAdam asked her the name of her attacker. Why on earth, then, didn't she immediately give it? Why, instead, did she trot out this stuff about Patricia being in danger? Because if Patricia was in danger, surely she could best be helped by Louise's revealing the identity of the criminal.

'Well, there seemed to me to be three possible solutions to this problem:

'(i) The person endangering Patricia was not the same person who had attacked Louise. I thought, on the whole, that that wasn't very likely, but it couldn't be ruled out, and I kept it in mind.

'(ii) It was Louise herself who endangered Patricia, and

now she was repenting it. That again postulated two criminals in the party.

'(iii) The remark was addressed to Richard Neame, who, as we know, was infatuated with Patricia, and would be certain, on hearing she was in danger, to go to her assistance. Even if he were disinclined for some reason to do so, *someone*, in view of Louise's urgency, would have to go, and public opinion would unanimously expect that someone to be Richard Neame.

'It was this last hypothesis which gave me most to think about. At the time, naturally, I'd no idea whether it was true or not, but I went on considering it, while still keeping an eye open for anything which might confirm either of the other two explanations.

'The interesting thing about it, to me, was that I couldn't for the moment see why Louise should want to send Richard Neame away at all. If it was he who had attacked her, there was no clear reason why she shouldn't denounce him instantly, and in his presence; after all, there were three other men there who might be considered competent to handle him. I seemed to be up against a blank wall.

'And then two things happened: I heard that Louise's maiden name was Benest; and a blackmail letter was discovered in her room.

'Immediately I remembered the main outlines of the Forrest case — the curious episode of the missing dagger. In the first place that gave me the motive, which so far had been missing: brother Andrew was taking his revenge for the execution of Edward Forrest — the knife slashes in themselves were evidence of definite hatred, and not of a crime committed, say, for the sake of money. And in the second place, Hadow, when he was narrating the Forrest case for the benefit of Wyndham and myself, let out one staggering, all-important fact.

'Louise Munro suffered from claustrophobia; she could not endure to be shut up.

'Now, cast your minds back to the Forrest case. Brother Andrew, and the missing dagger, weren't the only oddities in it. There was in addition one psychological inconsistency which couldn't be ignored. Charles Benest was a steady, unimaginative, reliable young man. Is it conceivable that such a person, even to protect his sister, would rush up behind a policeman and stab at him with what was practically a toy dagger? Of course not.

'When he admitted to doing that, Charles certainly wasn't shielding Edward or Andrew Forrest; obviously he was shielding Louise, who suffered from an affliction of such a nature that imprisonment would have driven her mad. Charles loved his sister so well that he was prepared to take the blame for what she had done, and so went to prison for fourteen years; and she, though she was devoted to him, *dared* not admit her guilt.

'One could guess fairly accurately what actually happened (and incidentally, Charles Benest has confirmed it since). It was Louise who picked up the dagger in the outer office. Then, you remember, Louise and Charles left the building, though they remained down below, hiding when the night-watchman went in. Then Louise went round to the courtyard – alone, it seems, while Charles waited in the alley – and witnessed the finding of the revolver and the murder itself.

Charles heard the shot. What, in the circumstances, would he do? Run away? Hardly; he wasn't that kind of man. He would – and he did – go up to the office. And Louise, running round from the courtyard to tell him what had happened, saw him go – and was in time, too, to see the policeman who shortly afterwards followed him. Plainly she was terrified in case her beloved Charles should seem to be involved in the murder. So she attacked the policeman. As you know, she was a much more hysterical character than her brother.

'No doubt she immediately threw aside the dagger, as Charles asserted that he did; and no doubt they were both very astonished when it wasn't found. It wasn't found, of course, because the "belated wayfarer" whom the constable saw had witnessed the entire business, and made off with it. And who could that belated wayfarer have been but brother Andrew?

'It's not easy at first sight to see *why* he took the dagger. But one's got to remember, I think, that he was – and will be, until he's hanged – a professional criminal. He saw the incident; he knew that the constable would not be able to identify the girl who attacked him; and consequently it was probable that the only evidence against her would be the dagger, with her prints on it, which she had so carelessly thrown away, and which would constitute, in his possession, a most agreeable weapon of blackmail. So he took it. He must have been considerably surprised when Charles confessed to the attack, but fortunately the value of the dagger was not thereby depreciated; he could still use it to blackmail Louise.

'Then Edward Forrest was tried, and Louise's evidence was instrumental in hanging him. For the moment Andrew

Forrest forgot about blackmail; he wanted revenge. He wrote Louise threatening letters, and on the day of Edward Forrest's execution he tried to kill her. She applied for police protection, and since he was cautious, and could afford to wait, he did nothing more for the moment. Time passed; Louise married a rich man; and it occurred to Andrew that before she was killed – and he still intended, with all his heart and soul, to kill her – she might as well be made, by his threatening to produce the dagger, to contribute to his private exchequer.'

Fen emptied his glass and refilled it. 'Most of that I was able to work out as soon as I heard of Louise Munro's connection with the Forrest case. I remember that even at the time of the trial I was assailed by vague doubts as to whether Charles Benest actually *had* attacked the policeman. And as soon as the blackmail note turned up in Louise's room, I was damned well certain that he hadn't.

'Wyndham, in the first instance, got the meaning of the note the wrong way round; he thought that it was from someone who was being blackmailed *by Louise*. But as it happened, the wording was quite ambiguous, and I'd no doubt what the proper interpretation was. "*I am tired of blackmail. You may expect a visit from me soon.*"

'Andrew Forrest had got all the money he wanted out of Louise; now he proposed to have his long-deferred revenge. You see why MacAdam said that Louise was frightened.

'So far, so good. And how did all this new evidence react on my three hypotheses regarding Louise's last words? Obviously it explained just why she wanted to get Richard Neame out of the way. She was devoted to Charles, remember; only a pathological condition of mind – claustro-phobia – induced her to let him go to prison in her place; and now she realised that she was dying, and her last thought was that the dagger must be preserved, her own guilt proved, and Charles released – his sentence, you know, had still seven more years to run. If she denounced Neame there and then, *he* would certainly not mention the dagger, and it might never come to light; if she spoke of it to the others in front of him, he might find a means of hiding or destroying it; it was possible, indeed, that he had provided against the con-tingency of arrest by arranging for some accomplice to do just exactly that – since he must have hated Charles Benest almost as much as he hated Louise. So she invented the tale about Patricia to get him away, relying on being able to tell the others about the existence of the dagger when he had gone. But she'd overestimated her strength. *"It mustn't be destroyed ... I'll tell you who ..."* And then she died.'

'But look here,' Noel interrupted, 'would he have *believed* such a tale?'

'There are three things to remember,' said Fen. 'First, that the previous attack on Patricia gave some plausibility to Louise's assertion; second, that Neame must have been abso-lutely staggered at finding his victim still alive, and have been incapable, for the moment, of lucid thought; and third, that in any case, he was glad of an excuse to get away. He must have expected to be denounced in the next few moments, and there might be a chance for him to make a dash for it in one of the cars. Of course,' Fen added parenthetically, 'Patricia was never in any danger at all.'

'The strychnine, though,' Janice interposed.

'Oh, Janice, don't you *see*?' Noel expostulated with some impatience.

'Be quiet, both of you,' said Fen waspishly. 'If you're not going to attend, we'd better abandon the subject altogether.'

'Oh, no, *please*,' Janice pleaded.

'Very well,' said Fen with obvious relief, 'I'll go on. I think we only need a brief account of what happened before, during and after the murder – now that the processes of detection have been exposed,' he added grandly.

'Andrew Forrest took the name of Richard Neame and got a job as a schoolmaster. While he was blackmailing Louise, he investigated, and insinuated himself into, her circle of acquaintances and friends. And the time came when MacAdam invited them both to the same house party at Rydalls. Neame knew that Louise would be there, since MacAdam was in the habit of informing people of their prospective fellow guests, and he came well-provided – among other things, with strychnine – for any emergency. On the previous evening, he had stayed at the same hotel as Patricia, and had typed his last note to Louise – the one we found – on the machine Patricia had borrowed from Peter Hadow.

'Louise arrived at Rydalls at practically the same moment as Neame and Patricia, and she must have seen the typewriter among Patricia's luggage. Shortly afterwards, Neame left his note in Louise's room – or perhaps pushed it under the door. Louise must have been very frightened when she found it; but she remembered Patricia's typewriter, and when Patricia had gone downstairs, Louise went to try it out. She found – as we found later – that the note had, in fact, been typed on that machine. What conclusions she drew, one doesn't know, but evidently she was anxious to find out more about Patricia. She took the diary as being the most likely source of information, and Patricia surprised her just as she was leaving. There was a scuffle, and Louise got away.

'Neame's opportunity came when the game of hide-and-seek was proposed. The house would be in darkness, and he would be able (so he thought) to time things very comfortably. He arranged to meet Louise in the long gallery, possessed himself of Nathan's gloves and a knife from the kitchen, and when the lights went out was ready for what he had to do. He can't, of course, have been aware of the presence of Simon Moore in the vestibule when he went through to the long gallery. He throttled Louise, and when, as he imagined, she was dead, mutilated her back with the knife. It must have been just after he had done this, and was preparing to leave – to be found, at the end of the game, in some other quarter of the house – that the first disaster (from his point of view) occurred.

'Hadow arrived; the gong was sounded prematurely; the lamp at the other end of the long gallery went on; and he heard you coming up on to the terrace.

'So he picked up the body of the woman he thought was dead, and kissed her. And when you two had gone, he flung aside the knife and gloves, and went to join the other guests in the drawing room. Since you stayed outside canoodling,' said Fen severely, 'he was able to get there well before you.

'Well, the search was organised, and he got his second shock: Louise was still alive. She spun her tale about Patricia, and he, no doubt, accepted it as an excuse for clearing out. But unfortunately, Simon Moore elected to go with him, and in the circumstances he couldn't give any excuse for leaving the house which wouldn't have made Moore instantly suspicious. He must have had a nasty few minutes before MacAdam came up to say that Louise hadn't, after all, named her assailant. In the meantime, of course, he'd seen through the purpose of Louise's Patricia fabrication. Louise's connection with the Forrest trial would come out soon enough, and perhaps the business about the dagger. He was prepared for that in any event, and if Louise hadn't had the chance to speak, there'd have been no more case against him than against anyone else without an alibi for the time of the murder. But she *had* spoken, and he thought he might divert suspicion from the real purpose of her words by giving the Patricia fabrication some basis in fact. He went into the bathroom and fetched out Patricia's bottle of tonic. He thought it had been poisoned, he said. And indeed, it had. He'd just that moment poisoned it himself ...'

There was a long silence. Then: 'Poor Patricia,' said Janice quietly.

'She'll get over it.' Noel spoke very definitely. 'There never was such an extrovert as that girl. The moment she finds anyone or anything else to interest her, Richard Neame will be completely forgotten – probably is already. What's happening about Charles Benest?'

'The dagger was found, of course,' said Fen. 'And he'll be released, after a lot of formalities. He'll get no compensation for the seven years he was in prison, because he pleaded guilty. But after all, they were only seven years of war – not so much loss.'

'I still can't understand it being Richard,' said Janice. 'He seemed so dull and ordinary.'

'I think he was a schizophrenic,' Fen answered, 'which means he didn't have to act the dullness and ordinariness. One half of him was the earnest educationist, the man who toiled and saved to send his brother to the university, the devoted lover of Patricia Davenant; the other half was a blackmailer, a swindler, and a murderer. It's a good thing that kind of person isn't born very often ...'

He poked inexpertly at the fire with the toe of his shoe. Depression was very perceptible on his normally cheerful features. 'It was an ugly crime,' he said. 'I think he'll hang – and from every point of view he deserves to ... Ah, well' – he reached for the whisky decanter – '*ad laetiora vertamus.*'

Losing the Plot

Catherine Aird

'What a truly magnificent view!' exclaimed Marion Carstairs. Like everyone else who entered the sitting room of the house on the hill at Almstone known as the Toft for the first time, she had crossed straight to the bay window and gazed out.

'It is indeed,' agreed Kenneth Marsden of Messrs Crombie and Marsden, Estate Agents and Valuers, of Berebury, 'although, as I am sure you already know, Miss Carstairs, you don't own the view from your windows unless, that is,' he added, 'you own that land as well.'

'Like dukes,' murmured Marion absently. 'They always made sure that they possessed all the land that could be seen from their mansions. After all, Capability Brown expected it of them.'

'Really?' said Kenneth Marsden politely. 'How interesting.'

'But this panorama is quite exceptional.'

'That's what everyone to whom I've shown the property says,' murmured the estate agent, finding that there was something about this lean, intelligent woman that made him pay more than usual attention to his grammar.

'You know, Mr Marsden, I do believe you can see the whole of the Alm valley from here.' Marion scanned the horizon. 'Isn't that Billing Bridge over there? I'm sure I came over the river that way.'

'It is,' said the estate agent, adding with professional caution, 'I am told that on a clear day you can see the spire of Calleford Minster.' He was well aware that those now following his calling had to be so much more circumspect in what they said in these days of rules and regulation than hitherto.

She was still looking eagerly out of the window. 'South, south-west – the sunsets must be a real joy up here too.'

'I'm sure,' said Kenneth Marsden quickly, 'but as it happens I haven't ever been here in the evening to see.'

She smiled. 'And I am hoping that I shall be here quite soon to do just that. You've got the address of my solicitors, haven't you?'

'There are, of course, other prospective purchasers who wish to see over the property.' He said this quite automatically, although in fact there had been very few and none of those were local. Miss Carstairs had come from London.

'Naturally. I quite understand that.' She turned back and said, 'Tell me, how could Mr and Mrs Boness have borne to move away from here?'

'Well, in a manner of speaking they haven't.' Kenneth

Marsden pointed out of the window. 'Do you see that little building down there to the left under the slope? It's called the Croft …'

'Toft and Croft!' exclaimed Marion Carstairs, clapping her hands. 'Of course! Toft and croft – that means the house and land on a hill in both Old English and Old Norse.'

'Well, they just moved into the Croft,' said Marsden, skating over the etymology.

'Keeping the view.'

'Exactly.'

'But,' she observed, pointing out of the window, 'if that wire fence over there is anything to go by, they've also kept the land right up to just in front of the Toft.'

'I am given to understand,' said the estate agent carefully, 'that Mrs Boness is quite a gardener and wished to retain as much of the original ground as possible.'

'Ah, I see …' All she could actually see were a few straggly wallflowers and an old felled birch tree.

'In fact, Miss Carstairs, as you will note from the title deeds, they did move their boundary back a little for the previous owners – the Mullens, they were called.'

'Oh, was there some trouble over it, then?' she asked swiftly.

'Mr Boness told me that it was to oblige the Mullens over some trees,' said the estate agent. 'They wanted them in their garden, not his. I believe, though, that Mr Boness had them cut down himself after the Mullens left.'

'But' – Marion Carstairs' eyebrows came up – 'I thought it was Mr Boness who is selling this house now. You hadn't told me that there had been someone else occupying it after them.'

'Oh, yes, but they were here only for four or five years. Michael Boness actually bought the place back from the new people, thinking he and his wife would move in again themselves.'

'But they didn't?'

'No. I was advised that in the end Mrs Boness decided she was quite happy where she was down in the Croft, and that's why they put the property back on the market.'

'Some gardeners like making new gardens and some don't,' observed Marion Carstairs. From what she could see of it, the garden of the house below had little to commend it besides the wallflowers but she did not say so. 'We're all different. That's the joy of being a gardener.'

The estate agent nodded. 'And, as you will have seen on your way in, there is still plenty of land with the property. It's just that it's on both sides of the house rather than in the front of it.'

'Oh, it's quite enough for my wants, Mr Marsden, I do assure you,' responded Marion Carstairs truthfully. 'Quite enough. And it's an alkaline soil, which is exactly what I am looking for.'

'Good. Now, if you'd like to see the other rooms ...'

It was early autumn by the time Marion Carstairs moved in to the Toft and was able to explore the garden properly for the first time. It was then that she took a really good look at the stretch of ground on her side of the wire fence opposite the bay window. What she saw was a row of sawn-off tree stumps, their remains now hardly visible above the grass. This had lain unmown through the summer months that the house had been on the market and it was now long and untidy.

On Michael Boness's side of the fence was a row of newly planted small young trees that had not been there when she had agreed to buy the Toft. The bed of the new trees extended almost exactly the length of her bay window.

'Leyland cypress, unless I'm very much mistaken,' she said to herself.

She said nothing to Michael Boness, though, when she met him in the village store, accepting his welcome to the Toft and Almstone with her customary reserved politeness.

'It's *Cupressocyparis leylandii*, Jean,' she told her sister later that week, when she telephoned her to report that she was settled in at the Toft. 'It'll grow a good three feet a year. What's that? Oh, yes, it'll be up to the level of the bay window in no time at all. And it's planted as densely as possible too. Just like the hedge that was here before. I reckon that he moved the boundary back when he got possession so that the stumps wouldn't be in the way of this new hedge.'

'Naughty,' said her sister.

'Clever,' said Marion.

She spent the winter preparing the ground for a spring planting of little Christmas trees. These she installed in the ground to the sides of the house and adjacent to the boundary fence, tending them carefully until they were properly established. A good horticultural specialist might have considered her a little unwise to put them in ground so very near a rapidly growing hedge of leylandii since this would all too soon take both light and moisture from the infant Christmas trees, but this factor did not seem to have occurred to Marion Carstairs.

Instead she seemed to be concentrating all her attention on the tree stumps.

'Now that I've had the stumps freshly cut I'll be able to kill them off before I have them taken out,' she called cheerfully across to Michael Boness when he appeared near her boundary one day when she was in the garden, carefully painting the fresh surface of each stump with a clear liquid. 'I'm sure they'll be so much easier to lift when they've died off completely, aren't you?'

'If anything you're using in the way of poison gets to the hedge on my side and damages it,' her neighbour began belligerently, 'you'll be in trouble, I can tell you.'

Marion Carstairs looked quite shocked. 'I shouldn't dream of letting that happen, Mr Boness. I promise you, I'll be very careful.'

'That's all very well,' Boness grunted, 'but I'll have you know that that hedge stays where it is, no matter what you say.'

'I shouldn't dream of saying anything, Mr Boness,' said Marion Carstairs in dulcet tones. 'Why should I? It's your hedge.'

'Because if,' he began heatedly and then fell suddenly silent.

'Your hedge is nothing to do with me,' went on Marion, still sweetly reasonable. 'The very idea ...'

At the end of her first year at the house, the leylandii was growing fast and thickening up well. All that Marion Carstairs had seen of Mr and Mrs Boness had been when she had called with the church choir singing Christmas carols.

'God rest you merry,' she had sung with the rest of the choir at their door. 'Let nothing you dismay ...'

By the end of Marion's second summer at the Toft Mike Boness's new leylandii hedge was beginning to show signs of interfering with the splendid view of the valley from her sitting room.

'I'm planning on having these old stumps out in the spring, Mr Boness,' she said one day when he was up near her boundary, examining his leylandii hedge.

'You'd better not disturb any roots on my side,' he said gruffly, 'or there'll be real trouble. That hedge stays.'

'Oh, I think we'll be able to get them out all right without doing any damage to your garden or mine,' she said.

'They're coming along very well now, these trees of mine are,' he said.

'They are indeed,' she said warmly.

'They're going to be fine, tall trees in no time at all.'

'I'm sure,' said Marion agreeably.

'Give me and the missus a bit of privacy in our old age, they will,' he went on, puzzled by her lack of reaction.

'They will indeed,' she said immediately. 'Just what you want as time goes by.'

'Doesn't help your view much though, does it?' Boness ventured slyly, watching her face.

'True,' admitted Marion Carstairs, 'but then I've always thought Goethe got it right.'

'Who?' he asked suspiciously.

'Goethe. A German poet.' Marion waved an arm over the valley. 'He said that no one could look at the view for more than fifteen minutes.'

'Did he?' Michael Boness sounded baffled. 'You do know these trees could get to more than a hundred feet if they're not trimmed?'

'Really? Do take care, won't you?' said Marion solicitously. 'You wouldn't want to fall off a ladder …'

'I'm not going to fall off a ladder,' he said crossly, 'because I'm not going to trim them.'

'Ah, then you won't need to worry about falling, will you?' she said.

She duly recounted the conversation to her sister, Jean, over the telephone that evening. 'Poor man,' she laughed. 'He doesn't know what to make of me.'

'Poor nothing,' snorted Jean. 'He's waiting for you to go down on bended knee and beg him to cut the leylandii down so that you can have your lovely view back.'

'He's going to be disappointed, then,' said Marion Carstairs. 'I will ask him, of course, but not just yet.'

'So how are your Christmas trees coming along?' asked her sister.

'Slowly but well,' said Marion. 'Another twelve months should see them just right.'

'And his leylandii?'

'Just wrong,' said Marion. 'For him, I mean. Fomes spreads underground along the roots at about a yard a year.'

'I'm very happy to hear it …' She stopped. 'But, Marion, won't it look very odd if the whole of his hedge is attacked by it at once?'

'Ah,' said Marion mysteriously, 'I've thought of that. And

about what to do if he gets on to someone about the fomes, as I'm sure he will.'

'I hope you have. After all, dear, fungi – what did you say the Latin name for fomes was?'

'*Heterobasidion annosum* ...'

'Even ones with outlandish names like – er – that don't usually travel in straight lines – and you know that, even if Mike Boness doesn't.'

'Ah,' she said, 'don't forget that the source of the infection – the old tree stumps – is in a straight line too.'

'But surely you don't want him ever to know that that's where it's come from.'

'No, of course not. That's why I had the stumps out and the ground grassed over ... Nobody will know they were ever there and as sure as eggs Michael Boness isn't going to tell anyone.'

'Why not?'

'For one thing, when he's had it spelled out to him, his estate agent won't like to hear what his client has been up to.'

'Go on ...'

'But it could be argued,' Marion said cogently, 'that recently planted trees such as his leylandii are unusually susceptible to that sort of infestation.'

'I do hope,' said Jean piously, 'that you don't have to argue anything.'

The next winter passed. This Christmas-tide the church choir sang the carol 'The Holly and the Ivy' at the front door of the Croft. When the choir came to the line 'When they are both full-grown' Michael Boness managed not to meet Marion Carstairs' eye.

It was high summer when Marion started to see early signs of disease in the leylandii hedge, which was now both thick and tall. That was when Marion first asked Mike Boness if he would consider lowering his trees so that she could have her view back.

'I thought you'd ask one day,' he said, grinning unpleasantly. 'All that talk about not minding what you looked at was hot air.'

'It's making my sitting room quite dark too,' she said meekly.

'That's your problem,' he said.

'Oh, dear.' Marion gave what she hoped was a womanly sigh. 'I really don't know what to do next.'

'You can't do anything,' he said roughly. 'It's my hedge, not yours. I can plant it wherever I like and let it get as high as I like, and neither you nor anyone else can stop me, no matter what you say.'

'But ...'

'And,' he added, 'since you've probably already thought about asking him, neither can your solicitor. They're clever, all right, but not that clever.'

'No.' She sighed again. 'I suppose not ...'

'So you might as well save your breath and your money.'

'And that's your last word, is it?' she asked.

Mike Boness paused and seemed to consider this. 'Well,' he drawled eventually, 'I dare say I could buy the Toft back from you if I had a mind to.'

'Buy it back?'

'That's if you were prepared to agree to my price, of course.'

'You mean you would really like to have it back again?'

'Only if the price was right, naturally.' He sniffed. 'It's not worth anything like what you gave for it, I can tell you.'

'Really?' she said.

'Not without the view.'

'I suppose you're right.'

He waved an arm over the valley. 'But with it ... then, that's different, isn't it?'

'Very,' said Marion Carstairs drily.

'Think about it,' he said.

'I will,' she promised.

'Mind you, I won't pay a lot.' He twisted his lips. 'But you're not going to get too many people willing to take the Toft off your hands now.'

'Not without the view,' she conceded gravely.

She was highly amused, though, when she described the encounter to her sister. 'What? No, we didn't talk money. It's a bit soon.'

'Soon for what?' enquired Jean.

'My Christmas trees. I'm waiting for the valuable seasonal trade, remember ...'

'Of course.'

'And for the damage from the fomes to be quite apparent.'

Marion Carstairs was all sympathy the next time she saw Mike Boness. 'Your poor hedge, Mr Boness. It has got something nasty, hasn't it? I do hope you weren't hoping to use it for timber.'

'I've got an expert coming to see it,' he said thickly, 'and if he tells me that it's anything you've done to it, then I'll be taking the matter further.'

'Me?' protested Marion. 'I haven't been near your hedge.'

'He's a proper tree specialist.'

'Just what you need,' she said.

'He'll know, and then watch out.'

'If I've done anything,' she corrected him.

'We'll see about that,' he said, storming away, red-faced. 'For my money, you'll be hearing more about this.'

Marion watched the arboriculturist come and go from behind her bedroom curtain. The one thing she didn't want at this stage was to be recognised. She was pleased, though, to see the expert look long and hard over the fence into her garden and then go over to peer equally hard at and dig round the remains of a felled birch tree on Mike Boness's land. That was after he had taken some samples of soil and of a fungus that had made its appearance on some of the leylandii roots. He took a core sample too from the stem of one of the dying leylandii trees.

'A textbook examination,' she reported to her sister, metaphorically rubbing her hands. 'Any minute now he'll be telling Boness about the fomes and that the spore could have come from that old birch of his. Birches are very susceptible to fomes too.'

'Like leylandii and Christmas trees,' observed her sister happily.

'Exactly. Now, I think our time has come … How much did you say you and Paul lost when you sold the house back to Boness, Jean?'

The sum of money named by Jean Mullen formed the basis of a claim by Marion Carstairs, the retired professor of plant biology at the Toft, against Michael Boness, the owner of the Croft, for damage to a substantial crop of *Picea abies* – otherwise known as Christmas trees – by a fungus called fomes, caught from his leylandii trees.

It was successful.

And without coming to court either.

The Christmas Train

Will Scott

'You're sure of your facts, Maxwell?' Mr Jeremiah Jones enquired.

'Positive, sir,' replied the sober Maxwell. 'Mr Hadlow Cribb landed this morning at Southampton. He has the jewels with him. Forty thousand pounds' worth. The trouble is, you can't get that lot through the Customs without somebody getting to know. And I got to know. It cost a bit!'

'Luxuries,' reflected Mr Jones, with a grin, 'are always expensive. But go on.'

'Mr Hadlow Cribb leaves Liverpool Street tonight for his country home at Friars Topliss where he intends to spend Christmas,' Maxwell proceeded. 'The jewels, of course, go with him. The train is due out at fourteen minutes past six.'

'Four hours,' murmured Mr Jones, with a glance at his watch. 'Busy train. It won't be too easy. Still, nothing ventured, nothing gained. I wish I'd had a little experience of this kind of work.'

'I ought to add,' Maxwell resumed, 'that Mr Hadlow Cribb was accompanied up from Southampton by Marks.'

'Marks?' Mr Jeremiah Jones' eyebrows lifted quickly. 'The new fellow in Beecham's office?'

'Exactly,' said Maxwell with a sigh.

'Scotland Yard protection! No, it isn't going to be too easy,' Mr Jones repeated. 'Can you get word to Dawlish?' he added as he reached for the telephone.

'Dawlish?'

Mr Jones nodded.

'You mean – as it were – put him wise?'

'Very wise, in a tactful way.'

'I might,' said Maxwell doubtfully.

'Aren't you sure?'

'I'm positive,' said Maxwell.

'Right. Then go and do it. Meet me here at five-thirty. Have everything ready – most important – mind you've got a bag that's as near as blow it to the one Mr Hadlow Cribb will carry his jewels in.'

'It shall be done,' Maxwell promised. And away he went.

Mr Jones unhooked the receiver.

'That Scotland Yard?' he was saying presently. 'Inspector Beecham? Say Mr Jones – an old friend!'

A minute passed and then a sly smile spread across Mr Jones' cheerful face.

'That you, Beecham? How are you? Merry Christmas! Well, why not? Peace on earth, goodwill to all men, and that kind of thing.

'Listen, Beecham, my own – I've a Christmas box for you. You remember I promised you, if I could get it, the – er – inside dope, as it's called – crude expression, I know, but it *is* called that, isn't it? I thought you'd know ... My dear fellow, I *am* getting on with it; do let me finish ...

'About that hold-up at Clapham the other week, when the girl was knocked out. You know how I hate brutality. I mean, he could have drugged her quite as easily, couldn't he? ... But I'm telling you! I've got your man, address and everything.

'Listen, I shall be in the Baltic at four ... No, no, Beecham, dear, I'd much rather see you personally ... It's your face. It brightens my day. Baltic at four. Better write it down. You're *so* forgetful!'

After which Mr Jones, with a happy chuckle, hooked the receiver, went to Liverpool Street, bought a couple of first-class train tickets, and proceeded to his accustomed corner in the dim saloon of the Baltic Hotel, off Piccadilly.

Promptly at four o'clock the stolid face of Detective Inspector Beecham of Scotland Yard appeared in sight, and the Scotland Yard man took a seat beside Mr Jones without a word.

'Compliments of the season!' said the latter brightly.

Beecham grunted.

'Cheer up!' Mr Jones beamed.

'You owe me some information,' Beecham reminded him.

'I have it here,' said Mr Jones, producing a pocketbook, which he placed on the table.

'When I say *owe* I mean owe,' Beecham added. 'Don't imagine you're paying off a debt. You're merely paying off arrears. You've slipped through my fingers so often that I take this without hesitation. I've a right to it. But it wipes nothing off. If I can get you tomorrow, I'll get you!'

'Why not tonight?' Mr Jones smiled.

'The first chance I get,' Beecham growled.

Mr Jones pulled a slip of paper from his pocketbook and began to unfold it. If he heard the suppressed gasp at his side he took no notice of it. He proceeded to unfold the little slip. But it wasn't the slip that had caused the Scotland Yard man to gasp. It was the sight of the two railway tickets. First class. To Friars Topliss.

'Here's the address,' said Mr Jones, passing the slip to the detective. 'You'll find your man there. You'll find the evidence too. And he richly deserves what's coming to him. You can tell him I said so, if you like, when you explain I obtained the information against him and so did your job for you.'

'Anything else?' asked Beecham.

'Nothing,' said Mr Jones, 'unless you'll let me call the waiter again, so that we can toast each other in the true festive—'

'I'll be going,' said Beecham curtly as he rose.

'You have a heart of stone, dear Beecham,' sighed Mr Jones. 'And yet, on Christmas Eve, when you see your stocking and the chimney shaft – who knows?'

But Detective Inspector Beecham was already on his way to the door – and Scotland Yard.

Back in his office the big man rang a bell and summoned his new assistant Marks to his side.

'Ah, Marks,' he said crisply. 'About Mr Hadlow Cribb. He's being accompanied tonight on the train?'

'I'm going myself, sir,' said Marks.

'You needn't trouble,' Beecham grunted.

'Not trouble, sir?'

'*I'm* going, myself!'

And as Beecham pecked the end off a big cigar he almost smiled his self-satisfaction.

The six-fourteen out of Liverpool Street faced the snow before it started. The snow blew in through the open end of the great building, covering the front of the engine and the sides of the passengers and the friends who were seeing them off. It was agreed by the majority that the weather was seasonable, but the vote was unanimous that the journey was certain to be long and uncomfortable.

In the laughing, grumbling, cheerful and anxious holiday crowds a small greyish man passed unnoticed. The cheerful ones were too cheerful to take the slightest interest in a figure so small and grey; the anxious ones too anxious. He passed through to the train as though he and the inconspicuous black bag he carried did not in fact exist, and when he sank wheezily into the corner of a first-class compartment that compartment still seemed empty.

Whereas everybody, cheerful or anxious, had at least one glance to spare for the tall and handsome Mr Jeremiah Jones, who, with the grave and dignified Maxwell at his heels, strode along the platform with an assurance which implied that if he had not bought the station at least he had a ten-day option upon it.

But since nobody had noticed the first greyish man, nobody noticed now that the inconspicuous black bag which

Maxwell carried in the wake of Mr Jones was the very twin brother of the inconspicuous black bag which the greyish man had carried a few moments before.

Except, that is, just one eager watcher with a black half-moon moustache, who now moved out of the obscurity of a dark corner and passed through the barrier not twenty feet behind Mr Jones and Maxwell.

Mr Jones and Maxwell passed the first-class compartment in which the greyish Mr Hadlow Cribb sat with his forty thousand pounds' worth of jewels, walked on until they were beyond the dining car and then selected a first-class compartment of their own.

But the eagerly watchful Detective Inspector Beecham had a few quiet words with the guard at the other end of the train and sank back into obscurity once more, this time in the shadows of the guard's van.

The train moved out of the station and Detective Inspector Beecham moved out of the guard's van together. The train moved out into the unfriendliness of the winter night, but Beecham moved out into the comparative cosiness of the corridor. This he traversed as far as the second coach where, having satisfied himself that Mr Hadlow Cribb was still alone and his shabby case unmolested, he took up his stand round the angle of the passage at the end of the coach and watched.

Mile succeeded mile, minute succeeded minute. Detective Inspector Beecham began to grow restless. The corridor windows were coated with snow. There was nothing to see and as little to do. Cheerful Christmasy shouts reached his ears from the ends of the train. He began to feel out of it. He began to feel bored. He shook himself and set out to walk the length of the train.

He passed through the dining car. He passed through two coaches beyond the dining car – satisfied that neither Mr Jones nor Maxwell had seen him do so – before he pulled up, again round the angle of a passage at the end of a coach.

Again he had perforce to play a waiting game. Again he began to feel out of it and bored. But at last, about an hour out of Liverpool Street he was pleased to hear a door slide down the corridor and thrilled to see that the two men who came out of the first-class compartment and made off in the direction of the rear of the train were Mr Jones and Maxwell. And Maxwell carried the second shabby little bag.

'Ah!' said Beecham softly to himself.

He let them get round the angle at the end of the coach; then he followed. He followed them through the next coach. He gave them three-quarters of a minute, then he plunged into the dining car prepared for the interesting bit in the rear section of the train.

But there he stopped.

And there Mr Jones stopped, too. Stopped ordering turkey and Christmas pudding to stare up at Detective Inspector Beecham and exclaim:

'Why, look who's here! Who could have thought it? Maxwell – wish the gentleman a merry Christmas!'

'A merry Christmas to you, sir,' said Maxwell, with a respectful dip of the head to the detective.

'Sit down and join us,' Mr Jones invited. 'After all, it only comes once a year and you can mutter "Without prejudice" under your breath as you drink my beer. Or shall it be port?'

Beecham sank wearily into the comfortable chair opposite the pair of them.

'I—' He stopped.

'Yes, dear fellow?' Mr Jones prompted.

'Nothing,' the detective mumbled.

'Don't tell me you're going away for Christmas,' said Mr Jones. 'I understand you don't believe in such tosh. Or am I wrong? Does that hard face of yours hide a heart that weeps after three glasses of rum punch and the sight of a holly berry?'

'The point is where are *you* going?' Beecham demanded.

'I don't see that's the point at all,' Mr Jones smiled. 'Waiter – or should it be steward? I travel so little – bring my friend Detective Inspector Beecham, of Scotland Yard, turkey and plum pudding and all things seasonable to eat and drink. Beecham, I don't think you know the steward, do you? The steward – Detective Inspector Beecham. Of Scotland Yard, you know. My very good friend.'

The attendant departed smiling, while the detective, with a neck going steadily pinker, attempted the futility of looking out of the window.

'When I want to advertise …' he said fiercely.

'You never will,' Mr Jones assured him. 'Too well known to need it. Too deeply established in the affections of the multitude to require such a cheap device. Advertise? You? When you have to, civilisation will have perished. What about the skating prospects for the holidays? I'd like your opinion.'

'What I'm never sure about,' said Beecham, turning a fierce glare on Mr Jones, 'is whether you're a crafty fool or just a fool.'

'Shall we say a lucky fool?' suggested Mr Jones.

'Luck, yes!' snapped Beecham.

'That shows,' said Mr Jones, 'how little you know me. You must get to know me better. Call round some time. Second Thursdays, you know. Tea. *And* cakes.'

To give the grim old man of Scotland Yard his due he almost enjoyed the turkey and plum pudding and the port that followed.

Despite his company he would have enjoyed the unusual evening entirely had it not been for the business which found him there. As it was he said little. Nor did he do more than listen occasionally to the ceaseless flow of light-hearted chatter which poured from the lips of Mr Jones.

He gave himself up to a waiting game and tried to calculate the number of miles that had pounded themselves out under the wheels of the train.

Mr Jones glanced at his watch.

'Eight o'clock? The snow's keeping us back. We were due in at Friars Topliss at five minutes to, surely?'

Beecham looked up at the mention of Friars Topliss, but still he said nothing. Mr Jones offered a cigar, which was refused, and then lit one himself.

Ten minutes later the train began to slow down.

'Now where are we?' said Mr Jones.

All down the dining car there was much rubbing of steamed windows, which answered no questions. An attendant, laden with Christmas fare on a tray, passed quickly.

'Tell me, steward, where are we?' Mr Jones enquired.

'Running into Etching Vale, sir,' replied the attendant. 'Friars Topliss in twenty-five minutes.'

'Thank you,' said Mr Jones, and turned to Maxwell.

'This is where we get off,' he said. 'Got everything, Maxwell?'

'Everything, sir,' Maxwell answered.

'Don't forget the bag.'

Maxwell stopped and picked up the shabby bag.

'Here it is, sir.'

Mr Jones rose. Maxwell rose too. Beecham stared, dissatisfied with he knew not what.

Maxwell helped Mr Jones into his big overcoat, pulled on his own and waited. Mr Jones pulled his hat down over his ears and turned up the collar of his coat.

The train stopped.

'Well, goodbye, Beecham, dear fellow,' Mr Jones said breezily. 'And, if I don't see you before, a Happy New Year.'

And out to the snow-covered platform he went, with Maxwell and the shabby little bag after him.

Beecham blinked. That little bag … Was it possible? Even before Hadlow Cribb reached the train? Or, by some trick, while he, Beecham, had been waiting his chance in the guard's van?

'Crafty, but I wonder if he's *really* a fool?' he thought solemnly.

The driving wind covered Mr Jones and the faithful Maxwell with snow in the twinkling of an eye. They dashed across the bleak platform of Etching Vale to the shelter of the station wall. And under this shelter they hurried to the barriers. Here Mr Jones offered two tickets.

The collector peered at the tickets in the doubtful lamplight.

'Pardon, sir,' he said, 'but this is Etching Vale.'

'Remarkable how you can tell, with all this snow on it,' remarked Mr Jones.

'These tickets are for Friars Topliss, sir,' said the collector.

'I know,' said Mr Jones, 'but I've changed my mind. I thought I'd get off here. It sort of called to me.'

'Not allowed to break the journey, sir,' the collector reminded him. 'I'm afraid you'll have to pay again.'

Mr Jones thrust a note into the collector's hand.

'Take it out of that,' he said, 'and buy your wife something for Christmas out of the balance.'

'No wife, sir,' the collector grinned.

'Soon will have,' Mr Jones assured him, 'with such charm as yours.'

He passed out into the snow-covered station square of Little Etching Vale, the soft footfalls of Maxwell on his left and, as he soon realised, other soft footfalls on his right. He turned and there once more was the stolid figure of Detective Inspector Beecham.

'Not again!' he exclaimed. 'But, my dear Beecham, I thought you were going on?'

'I thought you might be, too,' said Beecham.

'I changed my mind,' Mr Jones informed him.

'I changed my mind,' retorted Beecham.

'A costly process, I found it,' said Mr Jones.

'I didn't!' said Beecham.

'Oh, well, of course, you're known to the police,' said Mr Jones, 'which makes a difference!'

He smiled and waited, but Beecham waited too.

'Where now?' he asked.

'Where would you like to go?' said Beecham.

'You don't mean, do you, that the drinks are now on you?' said Mr Jones. 'But Beecham, my own, this is too touching! Very well – there's a decent-looking old-fashioned hostel over there. Shall we?'

'Anywhere,' growled Beecham.

They crossed the square to the old-fashioned hostel where, to Mr Jones' surprise, the Scotland Yard man immediately booked a private room and ordered the drinks to be sent up there.

'If you'll join me,' he said to Mr Jones.

'Delighted,' Mr Jones agreed. 'Does Maxwell remain in the weather and hold the horses' heads?'

'There'll be room for the three of us upstairs,' said Beecham.

'What could be better?' said Mr Jones.

And upstairs they went, with a waiter and tray to follow them.

'Cosy,' remarked Mr Jones, when the waiter had left them and closed the door. 'Shall you be staying here long?'

'About as long as it will take me to go through that little bag of yours,' Beecham answered.

'Beecham!' Mr Jones gasped. 'I don't understand you.'

'You will,' said Beecham. 'I always thought you'd be too clever. You let me see your train tickets this afternoon. After that, I just had to take this trip with you. Hand over the bag.'

'You know, Beecham, my sweet,' said Mr Jones, 'really I don't think you have the right.'

'I can soon get that,' said Beecham. 'Please yourself, if

you want to waste time. You'll waste it in my presence, that's all.'

Mr Jones sighed.

'Maxwell,' he said, 'nobody trusts us. It's a suspicious world. Pass the little bag to the gentleman.'

Maxwell passed the little bag to the gentleman, and the gentleman, frowning, promptly dragged it open. Out fell pyjamas, combs and toothbrushes. Nothing else. Beecham clicked his teeth and looked up.

'Pockets, probably?' he said.

'No friendliness at all,' observed Mr Jones with a fresh sigh. 'Your pockets, Maxwell.'

Maxwell emptied his pockets. Mr Jones emptied his. The detective's complexion darkened. He turned once more to the little bag, fumbled inside it, threw it on the floor. His hands passed swiftly, but certainly, down the attire of the other two men; then, with a muttered exclamation, he picked up a telephone that stood on a corner table.

'Friars Topliss police, quick!' he shouted.

'You might tell me, sweet Beecham,' Mr Jones put in, 'what *is* on your mind.'

But Beecham didn't. He sat glaring at the instrument in front of his nose until there was a faint tinkle.

'Yes?' he roared. 'This is Detective Inspector Beecham of Scotland Yard. Is the six-fourteen from Liverpool Street — what? Good Lord! Battered up? But I saw him — the jewels? Gone! I'll come along!'

He dropped the receiver and spun round.

'Without having the faintest idea as to what is on your mind,' said Mr Jones, 'I think you must admit that

I never batter them up. I may have many failings, but *never* that.'

'I don't exactly know where you come into this,' snapped Beecham, 'but bear this in mind. I'll land you.'

'I doubt it.' Mr Jones smiled. 'You'd like to, I fear, but it's such a disappointing world.'

Beecham strode to the door.

'Say goodbye to the gentleman, Maxwell,' said Mr Jones.

And Maxwell said goodbye to the gentleman.

'Dapper' Dawlish, expert but unlikeable, let himself into his Baker Street flat and snapped on the lights. He was satisfied with himself and the world in general. Or, at least, he was until he snapped on the lights.

Then he found himself looking down the barrel of an automatic, and he changed his opinion of the world at once.

'Good evening,' said Mr Jones. 'Or morning. Or what is it? Travelling about the world in a snowstorm makes one lose one's sense of time.'

'Who are you?' snarled Dawlish.

'Doesn't matter in the least,' said Mr Jones.

'What do you want?'

'The jewels you stole from Mr Hadlow Cribb on the Friars Topliss train,' said Mr Jones. 'And I want them now. I've been waiting two hours without a fire. I'm depressed. And when I'm depressed I'm nasty. That bulge in your right pocket, I believe. Come on! One, two—'

Which was where 'Dapper' Dawlish threw in.

'I'm hanged if I see how you knew,' he grumbled.

'But, of course, I knew,' said Mr Jones. 'It was I who had

you put wise this afternoon that the stuff would be on the train.'

'You?'

'Mind, you wouldn't have stood an earthly chance if I hadn't been on the train to take their attention away,' Mr Jones added. 'They watched dear old Cribb and you'd never have got near him. Brains, my lad. That's what gets you to the top.

'Mind, *I* couldn't have got the things. I'm too popular with the CID. They won't let me out of their sight. Which is why I sometimes have to leave the labouring to others. Which reminds me.'

He opened the parcel of gems, separated one from the rest, and tossed it on the table.

'The labourer is worthy of his hire,' he said, with a smile. 'You'd have got two – or even three – if you hadn't battered him up. Battering-up is a thing I detest. Or, at least, I've always thought so. I may change my mind one day. Even this day. Try following me and see! Goodbye, Mr – Dawlish, the name is, I believe. Charmed to have met you. And a merry Christmas.'

The Carpet Bagger

Colin Dexter

He who is conceived in a cage
Yearns for the cage.

Yevgeny Yevtushenko, 'Monologue of a Blue Fox on
an Alaskan Animal Farm'

1

There were longish periods now when the A34 was quiet, almost completely free of the swishing traffic. Only up there along the lay-by, two 'Long Vehicle' lorries ahead, was there still any continuum of activity – where at the side of a converted white caravan a single electric light bulb illuminated MACS SNAX – Open 24 Hour's.

Though with little formal education behind him, Danny had still felt the itch to transpose that single apostrophe from the last word to the first when, three-quarters of an hour earlier, he'd walked along to the serving hatch and ordered a cup of tea and a Melton Mowbray pork pie. Two other drivers had stood there then, chatting in desultory fashion and intermittently stamping their feet, their white plastic cups of piping-hot tea steaming brightly in the cold air of that late-January night. But apart from swapping first names, the three of them had said little to each other.

Now, back in the cab of the furniture van, Danny began to realise how very cold he was. Yet he told himself that 'cold' was only a relative concept and was trying to convince himself that he was only *relatively* cold. As with many things in life, it was all a question of mind over matter. His feet *felt* bloody frozen – Christ, they did. But they weren't *really* frozen, were they, Danny boy? What if he were standing barefoot on the far North Pole? He'd always believed there was just that one square yard of ice and snow comprising yer actual North Pole, and no one yet had managed to persuade him otherwise.

There were two newspapers in the cab: the *Daily Telegraph* (oddly?) and a late edition of the *Oxford Mail*. And newspapers were super for insulation, everyone knew that. Just stick a few sheets all the way round between your shirt and your jumper ...

He looked at his wristwatch: half past midnight, just gone.

It had been most unlike him to make one mistake – let alone two – on such an important day. How stupid, in the first place, to have left his faithful old army greatcoat behind! And absolutely bloody stupid to have drunk more than a little too much that lunchtime, because more than a little had amounted to more than a lot and he had spent far more than he could really afford of his meagre savings.

At a service station just north of Oxford he had stopped to buy two litre bottles of spring water – as well as the *Oxford Mail* – prior to pulling into the next lay-by, just before the M40 interchange. It was a bit naive, he knew, but he'd always believed that considerable quantities of water must significantly, and soon, serve to dilute and thereby to diminish the alcoholic level in the human bloodstream. And so it was that, an hour earlier, he'd forced himself to swallow all that flat and tasteless fluid to the final drop.

How come he'd been so careless?

Nervousness partly; and partly the exhilaration of the chase – of the fox keeping a few furlongs ahead of the yapping hounds. Perhaps the fox wasn't really exhilarated at all though – just frightened. Like he was, if he were honest with himself.

Just a bit.

Yet as he now sat behind the steering wheel in the darkened cab, he couldn't really believe he'd find himself in much trouble with the police that night. He wasn't sure whether they *could* nick him for being over the limit in charge of a stationary vehicle. But they'd still need *some* reason for breathalysing him, wouldn't they? They'd have one if they spotted the number plate, of course. But that was a pretty unlikely possibility, he reckoned. He hadn't read much of the *Oxford Mail*, but he'd seen one of its front-page headlines – 'OXON POLICE "UNABLE TO COPE" WITH CRIME' – and at least that was a nugget of encouragement in a naughty old world. A vehicle, so it seemed, was stolen every something seconds in the Thames Valley region and that was very good news indeed – considerably lengthening the odds against him being caught.

No. There was something else that was worrying him much more: the wretched 'tachometer' just to the left of the steering wheel – a device (as he was now learning) that showed details of speeds and times, of stoppings and startings. He just couldn't *understand* the thing, that was the trouble. Nor the pile of paper discs, looking like so many CDs, that stood beside it – discs marked 'Freightchart', with lines and spaces and boxes for Name and Base and Destination and Cargo and Date and Mileage and God knows what else. Confusing. Unfamiliar. He could gauge all the other risks all right; but not this one. Perhaps the police couldn't give him a random breath test. But could they give him a random tacho test?

He switched on the dimmish light in the roof of the cab and picked up one of the white discs, noting that two lines had already been completed, presumably in the cheap blue Biro that lay beside the pile: 'Smith, John; Southampton'.

Danny shook his head; and turned to the *Oxford Mail* again.

The main editorial picked up the page-one article on car-related crime, and Danny smiled to himself as he read the last few sentences:

The truth is that some of us, especially in the present cold snap, find it difficult enough to start our cars anyway – in spite of the considerable advantage of possessing our own car keys. So how is it that even some comparatively incompetent car thief can enter our vehicles in a matter of seconds, twist a couple of wires together (so we're told), and be seen two minutes later outpacing a pursuing police car along the nearest motorway? Come on, you manufacturers! Let's have a bit more resource and ingenuity in a fully committed nationwide crusade against this growing social evil.

Danny inclined his head slightly to the right and wondered what exactly the manufacturers *could* do – given the nature of electric current. And already it was considerably more difficult than the editor was suggesting. Four minutes it had taken him with this particular van at Southampton – a ramshackle heap that'd have about as much chance with a police car as a moped would with Nigel Mansell.

Brrr ... was it cold, though! And getting colder.

He could have turned on the engine for a quarter of an hour or so, but he was reluctant to waste any diesel. There was a long journey north ahead of him; and while he reckoned he'd be safe enough on the busy daytime motorways, he didn't really want to stop again. At the same time he daren't drive any further, either – not until he'd had a few hours' rest; or kip, if he were lucky. Twice, only an hour or so since, he'd almost fallen asleep at the wheel, his eyes slowly drooping downwards ... and further downwards, until his head followed them, only – suddenly! – to jerk upright in panic as consciousness reasserted itself.

Death had never figured prominently among his deepest fears, but he'd hardly had much of an innings as yet. And with all that cargo sitting there just behind him, well, it would have been criminal – *extra* criminal – to take any needless risks.

Thinking of all that cargo, though ...

Why'd it taken him so long to think of it?

Earlier he'd leafed through the bundle of inventories and

invoices, and counted at least – what, eighty? – eighty or more oriental rugs and carpets from Turkey, from Persia, from the Caucasus, from places sounding like Something-stan, with prices ranging from £4,500 (several such from Isfahan) to the cheapest (huh!) at only a thousand or so apiece. Danny's skill at scoring for his local darts team had once been legendary and his mind dwelt lovingly now on those accumulated spondulicks.

But the carpets weren't just precious, were they? They'd be *warm* too. Climb into the back, lie down under a couple of those beautifully embroidered beauties and – like his mum used to say – he'd soon be as snug as a bug in a rug.

A Persian rug.

There was no key to be found for the rear doors, but opening locks was Danny's hobby; his specialism. Some few people, he knew, could finish a fiendish crossword puzzle in a matter of minutes; a few others could spot a master move to some complex chess problem in hardly any time at all. And he was like that with opening locks.

Only quicker.

And immediately disappointed.

Inside, no neatly laid-out pile of carpets presented itself for him to lie on, like the princess on the mattresses. Instead, facing him, from floor to ceiling, lying lengthways along the sides of the van, stood a honeycomb of tightly pack-aged carpets rolled up in their thick cardboard cylindrical wrappings. Jes-*us*! Even with an outsize Stanley knife it'd probably take him half an hour to liberate only *one* of them. And he couldn't just slide one out and carve it up in the middle of the lay-by, now could he?

Aagh! Forget it.

He walked back, clambered up the two metal footholds, and sat once more in the front cab, now grown even chillier. One bit of luck, though. The *Daily Telegraph* proved to be a pretty substantial broadsheet, and he was dividing the multi-paged wodge in half when he spotted the headline, in the Home News section, and was soon reading the article beneath it:

TRUSTY ABSCONDS

Wiltshire Police report the escape of Daniel Smithson from Winchester Gaol, where most recently he was serving a four-year sentence for robbery.

For the last three months it appears that Smithson had been privileged to enjoy the maximum range of freedom within the prison regime, and indeed during the past week had been working in a garden adjacent to the prison with a brick wall only some four feet high separating him from the outside world.

Although prison authorities are unwilling to give specific details, it is understood that the ex-soldier Smithson, who for the last twelve years has seen little except the inside of a cell in one of HM prisons, was due for release shortly.

Aged forty-three, he is five feet seven inches in height, of slim-to-medium build, and has shortish brown hair. Lightly tattooed on the back of the lower knuckles of the left hand are the letters I – L – Y – K, supposed by fellow prisoners to commemorate a former girlfriend: 'I Love You Kate'.

The escapee has no record of any criminal violence, and it is the view of the prison officers at Winchester that he poses no threat whatsoever to the public at large. An early re-arrest is expected.

Characteristically, Danny tilted his head to the right, and glanced through the article again. Then nodded to himself. There *were* people who couldn't cope with life outside the Rules and Regulations of an institution – just as there were people (hadn't he just read it?) who couldn't quite cope with all this crime. And it was easy to read between the lines of that last couple of sentences, wasn't it? 'No need to clap the darbies round the poor sod's wrists. Nah! He'll probably soon be knocking on the gates o' the nearest nick hisself.'

Funny old business, life. Full o' pitfalls – full of opportunities, too. Just watch out for the first – and make sure you grab hold o' the second. Common sense, innit? That's what his dad had told him.

Danny clasped his hands, left over right, and rubbed them vigorously together against the numbing cold. And even as he did so, he found himself looking down at the lower knuckles of his upper hand.

2

'I coulda scored the bloody thing in me carpet slippers, honest I could.'

'You reckon?'

'And if Oxford hadn't buggered up that last-minute penalty—'

'You'da won a fortune.'

'Third divi on the treble-chance.'

'About sixpence.'

'We've gone decimal, Sarge – remember?'

PC Watson accelerated up the slip road into the A34 (N) from the Pear Tree roundabout, noting as he did so the miraculously civilised deceleration of a couple of cars behind him.

'Better take a gander somewhere, I s'pose,' suggested Sergeant Hodges a couple of miles further on, pointing to one of the several lay-bys on the twin-track road that led up to the M40 interchange.

No snack bar here. Just the black hulks of two juggernauts; and tucked in behind them an old man in an old car studying an old map.

'Need any help, sir?'

'No!'

Sod you then, thought Watson, as he moved forward past the two container lorries.

At the far end of the lay-by – not spotted earlier – was a Jaguar of indeterminate colour: 'indeterminate' partly because during the hours of darkness light reflected oddly from the metallic sheen of some cars; and partly because Watson was in any case wholly colour blind between the reds and the blues.

But he made no further advance as he saw the grey head of the driver jerk round and the dusky-headed young maiden beside him hasten to fasten up the buttons on her blouse.

'Any joy?' asked Hodges.

Watson shook his head as he got back into the car. 'Well, 'cept for the fellow up front there in the Jag, perhaps.'

Half a mile or so further along, Hodges nodded again to his left, and this time the Vauxhall Senator pulled in behind a furniture van.

'Coffee for me, Barry. Not too much milk, and two sugars, please.'

But Watson was no more than a few seconds into his mission before he stopped and stared. When (only an hour since) he'd glanced through the briefing files and the traffic telexes back in Kidlington Police HQ, the last three letters of one particular stolen vehicle had caught his notice. How otherwise? For those last three letters were the initials of his own name, Barry Robert Watson; and here, on the van in front of him, was the registration number C 674 BRW.

There was always an awful lot of luck needed in apprehending villains, Watson had already learnt that – unless you were looking for a ginger-bearded giant, with a wooden leg, and a dinosaur tattooed on his balding head. And this *was* a bit of luck. Surely so.

Back in the police car, Hodges rang through to the Control Room at HQ, where within only a few seconds an operator read from his Police National Computer screen that the said vehicle, reg. C 674 BRW, had been stolen earlier that evening in Southampton. The number had appeared in the Thames Valley briefing files only because there seemed to be some suggestion that the vehicle might be heading north. Along the A34. Up into Oxfordshire.

His head cushioned on his arms, the driver appeared to be deeply asleep, since only after a series of staccato raps on the cab window did he raise his head above the steering wheel.

'This your vehicle?' bawled Watson.

'Wha'?'

'Police!'

The driver slowly wound down his window. 'Wha's the trouble, mate?'

'This your vehicle?'

'Wha', this? I wouldn't have it if you gev it me!'

'Let's see your licence, please.'

'What licence?'

'Not your bloody *dog* licence, is it!'

'You got so many days on producin' yer licence, you know that.'

'Haven't got one – is that what you're saying?'

'Not on me, no.'

'What's your name?' (It was Hodges who took over now.)

'John Smith.'

'Sorry, yeah. Shoulda known.'

'Anything else I can help you with?'

'You'd better get down and come along with us.'

'Have I got any option, mate?'

'Not much.'

'Hold on a tick, then. I'd better just fill in the old tacho thing here. Got to keep yer records up to date, you know – 'specially if you get delayed a bit.'

'Yeah, well, let's say you look like getting delayed a bit.'

Beckoning Watson to the other side of the van, and with one foot now on the lower foothold, Hodges raised himself to look into the cab, where he saw the driver filling in a white tachometer disc – writing slowly and innocently enough with a cheap blue Biro.

The driver of the lorry in front walked back to the van.

'Everything OK, Officer?'

Hodges nodded and stepped down. 'No problems.'

'Everything OK, Danny?' continued the other, as the cab door now opened.

'Fine, yeah! Just forgot me licence, din I?'

'"Danny", eh?' remarked Sergeant Hodges as he steered the man into the nearside rear seat of the Vauxhall, conscious that the slimly built, quietly spoken man beside him hardly fitted the stock profile of any tearaway joyrider.

'Yeah! What do we call you?' added PC Watson over his shoulder.

'"Mr Smith"?' suggested Danny quietly.

3

If the Custody Suite at Bicester Police Station is not a match for the British Airways Club Class lounge at Heathrow, it is at least a well-lit, well-ventilated room – separated from the cell area, and affording its present occupant a comfortable enough introit into his temporary detention.

In the presence of the arrested person himself (in the presence too of PC Watson), Sergeant Russell, the Custody Officer, standing in shirtsleeves at a tall desk, has recited the statutory 'Notice to Accused Persons', and is now completing the Custody Record, as the law requires of him. Russell is an older man, a stickler for procedure, and he fills in the lengthy sections with scrupulous care. He has already made the decision to authorise the continued custody of the prisoner.

'Let me just put it to you once more, lad. What's your real name?'

'Told you, din I? How many more times I got to tell you?'

Russell sighs wearily. There is little he can do if the man persists in such manifest falsehoods.

Yet Danny does so persist; has been so persisting for the

past half-hour – ever since he'd slid a letter addressed to him beneath the driver's seat in the front of the cab; ever since he'd jumped down into the strong arms of the law. Literally so.

'Still no news of your address?'

'No fixed abode, innit? Told you, din I? I'm a new-age traveller.'

'Occupation, then – "Traveller". OK?'

'Yeah.'

'And you travelled down here in a vehicle stolen from a depot in Southampton at approximately 9.35 p.m. yesterday evening, right?'

'Who told you that?'

'Relax! I've got to put *summat* down here, that's all – in the "Grounds for Detention" bit. Don't you understand that?'

Russell collects together his sheets of white A4, and prepares to call it a day. Or a night. 'I just hope the Southampton boys've got as much patience as I have, that's all.'

'Do we fingerprint him?' asks Watson.

'We do not! We follow the rulebook; and the rulebook says he's got the right to a nice hot cuppa, if he wants one.'

Danny very much wants one, for his mouth is dry. But he is suddenly frightened and in danger of losing his self-control.

'You can't bloody keep me 'ere!' The voice has grown harsh, the muscles are tightened in the neck. There is, for the first time since the arrest, a strong hint of a tightly coiled spring within the prisoner's sinewy frame. His head moves forward over the desk which separates him from his interlocutor.

'Constable!' Russell is fully prepared; he experiences no

fear, as he steps towards the door at the back of the room which leads to his office. 'Put the cuffs on him, will you? I shan't be more'n a minute or two—'

'No!'

As suddenly as it has appeared, the tension has now gone. The voice is quiet once more; the muscles once more relaxed. The man breathes out a long, deep sigh, then holds up his hands in a gesture of mock surrender.

And Russell steps back to the desk, lays down the Custody Record, and takes out his pen again.

'OK. Let's be having things, lad.'

Ten minutes later, from his own office, Sergeant Russell has introduced himself, and is speaking on the telephone to a senior prison officer at Winchester.

'You've got somebody there who's just scarpered, I think? Rather you *haven't* got somebody there, if you see what I mean. Name o' Smithson.'

'Oh God, no!'

'Pardon?'

'Just keep him, will you?'

'We *are* keeping him. He's here – at Bicester – locked in his cell.'

'Excellent! As I say, just keep him there.'

'What's *that* supposed to mean?'

'It means we don't want him back here, that's what.'

'I'm not with you.'

'Either keep him, or lose him, that's what I'm saying. Yes … Not a bad idea that, Sergeant. Why don't you just *lose* him, and do us all a bloody favour?'

There is a chuckle at the Winchester end of the line before the voice continues, in a more serious vein, to explain these strange rejoinders.

Daniel Smithson had joined the army at the age of sixteen, as a boy soldier; become a mercenary in Africa at the age of twenty-two; served in the SAS for six years after that; and then ... and then served somewhere else – in prison, for virtually the whole of the past twelve years, his offences ranging from petty theft to hefty larceny. *And* (and this was the real point) the magistrates and the judges and the prison authorities were all becoming increasingly undecided about how to deal with the fellow. What he'd do was this. He'd keep his nose immaculately clean, cause no trouble to anybody, and end up by getting a 'trusty' job. Then, well, he'd bugger off a day or two before he was due for release. Huh! Once outside, he'd pinch as much as his pockets could accommodate, nick a car, live it up for a few days; then (inevitably) get re-arrested, and return to his old haunts and his old mates, with the Prison Governor treating him like the Prodigal Son. The simple truth was that Smithson just couldn't settle down outside the prison walls: he needed – enjoyed! – the stable routine of a familiar nick. Though not a big fellow, he was a strong and wiry one, and his SAS history had reached the prison well ahead of him. No one buggered about (if that was the right word) with Mr Danny Smithson.

'Oh no, Sergeant. No one.'

One thing has been troubling Russell during the recital of the Winchester prisoner's CV: the fact that his man hardly looks the part of some ex-SAS paratrooper, or whatever; and Russell puts his thoughts into words.

'You sure we've got the right fellow – the fellow you're talking about?'

'Put him on the line, if you like. I'll soon tell you.'

'No, I don't think I can allow that.'

'Easy enough to tell, anyway. He's got some letters tattooed on the back of one of his hands – left hand, I think it is. They mentioned it in the papers. Hold on! Shan't be a tick.'

In fact four minutes drag by before the prison officer reads from a folder; and Russell listens carefully.

'I'll go and check straightaway. Shan't be a tick.'

Danny is not asleep. He sits on the side of the bed, staring at the floor – and looking up with no apparent interest as Russell unlocks the door.

'Just lift up your hands, will you, Danny Boy.'

The prisoner lifts up his hands as if, once again, he is surrendering to the foe.

'Good. Now turn your hands round, please.'

So Danny turns his hands round; and on the lower joints of the fingers on his left hand Russell reads the letters I – L – Y– K.

This time it is the Winchester end which has waited through four long minutes.

'Well?'

'Yep – it's him, all right. When'll you be coming to fetch him?'

'Not before breakfast, I'll tell you that! We'll let you know.'

'OK.'

'By the way, what exactly are you holding him on?'

'Theft of vehicle; theft of goods in transit; driving without a licence; driving without—'

'Same old stuff.'

'Same old sentence, like as not.'

'Unless some judge suddenly decides to show a bit o' sense and refuses to lock the silly sod away again.'

Russell is not prepared to enter any penological discussion, and prepares to sign off.

'Thanks anyway. Will you be coming yourself?'

'Me? God, no. I'll be seeing him soon enough.'

'And no handcuffs, you say.'

'That's it. No need. Let him have a stroll round Bicester after breakfast by all means – no problem. No cuffs, though. He's one of those who can't stand any physical contact with people. Know what I mean?'

'Doesn't sound as if he'll give us any trouble, anyway.'

'I wouldn't go quite so far as that.'

'What do you mean?'

'Nothing really. Just don't be surprised if he – well, if he strings you along a bit. Know what I mean? He's a bit of a joker is our Danny. Always was. Probably ask you for a bottle of champers for breakfast – say it's doctor's orders.'

'We do a nice little line in tea bags down here in Bicester.'

'Cheers then.'

'Cheers.'

PC Watson has finished his report, and now looks in for the last time at his prisoner.

'Anything you want?'

Danny shakes his head. 'Unless you'd like to gimme me Biro back.'

Returning to the Custody Suite, Watson passes on the request; and Sergeant Russell looks down, first at the cash envelope, then at the property bag – from the latter finally taking out the cheap blue pen with which Danny had written on the tacho disc.

'No harm, I suppose. He probably wants to write a poem on the loo paper.'

4

At 8.20 a.m. the minibus from Winchester arrived in the front yard of Bicester Police Station, where one of the two prison personnel immediately alighted and reported to the Information Desk.

Everything was ready.

Driven now into the yard behind the main building ('Police Vehicles Only'), the minibus was backed up alongside the wall, its rear window coming to a halt only a few feet from the single external door of the Custody Suite.

The prisoner had not after all ordered champers for breakfast; instead he had done splendid justice to the sausages and beans brought to him an hour earlier. Yet he did make one request when the cell door was again unlocked for his departure, just after 8.30 a.m. Two spare blankets were folded beside the bed, and he'd asked if he could have one to put round him on the journey. He had no overcoat; it was a cold morning.

198

Not very much to ask at all really, was it?

It had all happened so very suddenly that no one after-wards had any particularly clear picture of the events. But it went something like this ...

As he was walking through the exit door from the Custody Suite, the blanket which the prisoner was holding about his head and shoulders was dramatically whisked away and equally dramatically whipped over the head and shoulders of the tall, bearded officer who was about to unlock the nearside door of the minibus. Then, dodging lightly past him, the prisoner sprinted the thirty or so yards to the tall beech hedge which enclosed the rear yard. The hedge was strengthened by a six-foot meshed-wire fence – the fence, in turn, supported every six or seven yards by concrete posts. These posts were some five feet in height, finishing a foot or so below the top of the hedge. One of the posts – and only one – was itself strengthened by a concrete strut which formed an angle of forty-five degrees to the ground and which joined the post roughly halfway up, looking rather like a lambda in the Greek alphabet.

At full speed the prisoner leapt at this structure, his left foot landing firm on the top of the strut, his right foot equally firm on the top of the post; and then, propelled by such twin leverage, he had cleared the beech hedge by several inches, landing neatly on the grass of a school playing field beyond. Someone later said it was a bit like watching a Russian gymnast clearing a vaulting horse at the Olympics.

The prisoner was gone.

Neither of the heavy Winchester men could hope to match such a nimble-footed feat of levitation; and it was ten minutes before a wailing police car, forced to take the long way round the front of the station, was criss-crossing the maze of streets in the King's End estate behind, where (it was believed) the prisoner was last sighted.

But not sighted again.

5

The loo paper in the cells at Bicester may by no means be described as 'Savoy Soft', stiffly reluctant as it is to accommodate itself to the contours of the average human backside. Yet (as Sergeant Russell had earlier intimated) it makes unexpectedly fine writing paper; and it was two sheets of this paper which one of the cleaners found just before lunchtime that same day – between the folds of the remaining blanket in the cell which had housed the escaped prisoner.

The escape had caused no little embarrassment to the officers concerned, and (worse still) would almost certainly hit the national headlines the following day. Thus it was that Chief Inspector Page of Thames Valley CID (no less) had little compunction in summoning the now off-duty officers Russell, Hodges and Watson, to his office in Kidlington at 11 a.m. to review the matter – and the cleaner's discovery.

The spelling and punctuation were both a bit shaky, but the import of the letter could hardly have given a clearer answer to what had hitherto seemed the increasingly bewildering question of the escaped man's identity:

The Torygraph did it, very useful paper and a lot of criminals vote tory. It was Smithson give me the idea because we got the same name see. If he got nicked he gets good treatment but if I got nicked no, so what about him and me changing places for a little wile and no harm done is it? Besides, probably gives me a best chance of scarpering – lots of that now days, perhaps its the resession to blame like for every thing else. There was just that one problem, that tatoo I read about and when you coppers thought I was filling in the old tacko with the blue byro I was just writing out them four letters on the old nuckles see, easy! Then I done a pretty good job really with all that stuff about me name, dont you think so? Well well Danny Smithson boy, I wonder where you are, have <u>you</u> desided to keep out this time, why not?

I'll leave this letter in the bottom blanket because I've got ideas with the top one. If I get away what a big laugh for me when you find it, and if I dont its your turn for the big laugh

Samuel (Danny) Lambert

PS you can give me old comb and spare hanky to Oxfam or the Sally army, its up to you

Newly recruited to the Force, PC Watson was glad to have someone to chat with – even a subdued-looking Sergeant Russell – as they stood in the lunch queue in the HQ canteen.

'Rotten bit o' luck, Sarge ...' he began.

'You make your own luck, lad. I shoulda been far more careful checking out that tattoo.'

'I was thinking more about both of 'em being named "Danny".'

'*Nick*named, you mean – one of 'em.'

'Yeah. I mean, there's your "Pongo" Warings ...'

'And your "Nobby" Clarks ...'

'How come your "Danny" Lamberts, though?'

'Dunno.'

The queue moved a couple of feet, and the plainclothes man in front of them turned round to proffer a suggestion:

'Might be someone from Stamford? Stamford in Lincolnshire? Lamberts there often get called "Danny", after Daniel Lambert – fellow who weighed fifty-two stone odd – still in the *Guinness Book of Records*.'

'Who's *he* when he's at home?' asked Watson, after they'd been served.

'You don't know?'

Watson shook his head.

'That, my lad, was Chief Inspector Morse.'

Watson frowned slightly. He'd never heard of the man; yet for a fleeting second he'd thought he'd almost recognised the profile as that grey head had turned towards them in the queue ...

Next morning, the Governor of HM Prison Winchester received a full report on the case, now becoming widely known as the 'Cock-up at Bicester Corral', including a photocopy of the letter found in the escapee's cell. He immediately summoned the senior prison officer from D Wing, where Smithson had spent so many comparatively contented months and years.

'You'll be interested in this.' The Governor handed over the file.

Price, a thick-set Irishman, sat down and began reading.

'No news of our Danny?' interrupted the Governor.

Price shook his head. Then, halfway through the letter, his eyes suddenly widened with a new and startling notion.

'You don't think, sorr …?' he began slowly, pointing to the letter.

The Governor groaned, permitting himself also, albeit briefly, to contemplate the unimaginable.

'Don't tell me *that*! Please! Don't tell me it's *Smithson's* writing?'

Price studied the writing of the letter again. 'Yes, sorr. I'm sorry. But I'm pretty sure it is.'

And for a few moments the two men sat there in silence, each of them visualising their erstwhile prisoner perched aloft in the cabin of a stolen van, and carefully over-tracing his own tattoos with a cheap blue Biro pen …

A Hint of Danger

William Bankier

Carter Varley was accustomed to writing mystery stories, having them published, and then hearing no more about them. His friends seldom read one or, if they did, they kept silent about it. Varley considered this to be a kind of passive hostility motivated by envy. As for strangers – the anonymous public who were exposed to his work in various magazines – he supposed they turned the pages, were amused or not, and then went about the business of their lives.

But now, on this drafty November morning with a grey rain sweeping across Wimbledon Common and spattering against the window beside Varley's desk, here was an astonishing letter from America. It had been forwarded to him by the editor of a magazine published in New York, but the postmark was Chattanooga, Tennessee.

'Imagine my surprise,' the letter began, 'when I read your story entitled "Forgotten, Not Gone" and discovered it was about me!' The writer went on to identify himself as William Stoke (indeed the name Varley had invented for the villain in his story) and to say that, furthermore, he was a practising lawyer. This compounded the coincidence almost beyond belief because Varley's fictional Stoke had been a lawyer, too.

With an ethereal feeling Varley cranked paper into his machine and typed an answer. He apologised for any embarrassment and expressed his amazement at the sort of coincidence that happens in real life, too bizarre ever to be written into a story. Varley thanked Stoke for his letter and then, uncharacteristically, invited the American to call if ever he should be in London.

The rain stopped in early afternoon. Varley went out for a walk in the High Street, paid an outrageous price at the grocer's for some salad ingredients, posted his letter to America, and then went to the Dog and Fox for a pint.

Tucked away in a corner, his portly torso wedged into a leather armchair, the mug of brown ale glowing on polished oak easily within reach, Varley stared at the hissing glow of the gas fire and worried about what he had done. He did not want people dropping in on him, not friends, not strangers, certainly not an aggressive American who would think he had a claim on Varley simply because his name had fallen into the author's mind by sheer happenstance.

Varley drank the ale, making up his mind to have another. And perhaps a couple of those Scotch eggs. The crusty, breaded eggs improved his mood and so did the second pint. He was fretting for nothing. Stoke had written because he was surprised and pleased to see his name in print. Varley's reply was no more than proper, and the invitation was the sort of formality that nobody takes seriously. Chattanooga was a long way from London – nothing more would ever come of it.

Christmas arrived and Varley was forced to recognise that he had not got over the death of his wife two years ago. By burrowing like a mole into mountains of work, he could deceive himself for months at a time into thinking he was self-sufficient and secure. But when he lifted his head at the end of the year he encountered all kinds of ferocious reminders – the scent of oranges, frost in his nostrils on night walks, lights on trees seen through curtained windows, and at his doorway three children singing a carol.

Varley gave them fifty pence and sent them away, then turned out all his lights and sat shivering in the dark, drinking Scotch whisky and facing the past like a martyr submitting to the fire. He saw the old chapel with himself in his twenties, dressed in cassock and surplice on the tenor side of the chancel, holding his hymnbook high and looking across it at Beatrice in the front row of the altos. Midnight service on Christmas Eve.

Those had been the good years, the early days of his life with Beatrice. Time eroded the relationship until it became something no longer worth preserving. But now that he was going it alone, Varley's mind would only deliver up memories of sweet events.

The year finally turned and delivered a cold January followed by a grey wet February, both of which were improvements on the festive season as far as Carter Varley was concerned. Then came a surprisingly sunny March, milder than the month had been in a decade. These were ideal working days and he got his head down and tunnelled busily into the material of his experience.

Then the telephone rang.

Varley jumped, barking his knee on the desk and spilling milky coffee on the cherrywood surface. Leaving a paper napkin to absorb the overflow, he limped out of the study and into the bedroom, balancing the clamour of the bell with short angry responses.

'Yes. All right. Hang on.'

The voice on the line was, to Varley's ear, almost stage-American. 'Hello, this is Mr Billy Stoke speaking. Is that Mr Carter Varley?'

'Yes, it is.' Said with heart beginning to pound.

'I hope I'm not interrupting your work but we got into London last night and I figured that after the very kind invitation in your letter I had to call and say hello.'

'Yes, rather. Very glad you did.'

Stoke laughed in a boyish way. 'I don't suppose you get telephoned very often by a character in one of your stories.'

A few generalities were exchanged during which Stoke mentioned the name Irene. He was not travelling alone and, for some reason, this eased Varley's anxiety. Then the American said, 'I know you writers have a schedule to stick to, but I was hoping Irene and I might persuade you to come to London and have a meal with us.'

Varley had not ventured beyond the High Street in months. London meant the train to Waterloo, crowds, taxis, a strange hotel lobby. 'Yes, very nice. It's a question of time. Perhaps a day next week.'

'Afraid we're only in London for a couple of days. We've rented a car and we plan to drive along the south coast.'

A momentary silence. Then Varley was astonished to hear himself saying, 'Then come out here for dinner. Yes, by all means, come this evening.'

The American's pleasure at the invitation was so gratifying that Varley found himself going further. It was as if some hospitable impulse buried long ago had been uncovered. 'Look here,' he said, 'why don't you check out of the hotel? I have a perfectly good guest room here.'

That was the end of writing for the day. Varley set aside his current manuscript, took a fresh sheet of paper, and drafted a menu for dinner. Under it he listed the items he would have to buy at the shops, including wine and beer and a bottle of cognac.

By six o'clock the roast of beef, surrounded by potatoes, carrots and onions, was in the oven, filling the house with its appetising aroma. A litre of Italian red wine was uncorked and resting on the Jacobean sideboard. Varley admired the table setting – gleaming silver, polished plates, folded linen, four tall candles in antique brass sticks. A long time since he had drawn the oak table away from the wall and raised the drop leaves.

He was placing a few additional lumps of smokeless coal on the open fire when he heard the swing of the iron gate followed by the scrape of footsteps outside the front door. Varley paused at the hall mirror to adjust the knot in his tie and smooth the edges of his greying hair. There was colour in his face for the first time in a year and his eyes were clear and alert.

William and Irene Stoke from Chattanooga, Tennessee turned out to be everything Varley could have hoped for and nothing he might have feared. For one thing, they were not dressed in what he considered to be the style of children – no turtleneck sweaters, no peaked caps, no blazers with crests on them. Stoke, tall and heavyset, deeply tanned and handsome, ten years younger than Varley's half-century, was wearing a dark suit, white shirt, and modest tie. His shoes had laces and were polished black. Too good to be true.

Irene Stoke could not have been older than thirty. She had a stage beauty, regular features made up immaculately, hair like burnished copper worn in one thick braid over her shoulder, and classic eyes of penetrating green.

They sat with drinks in upholstered chairs drawn close to the fire while rain came out of the darkness and rattled on the windows. Billy Stoke said, 'Always wanted to see England but kept putting it off. It was that nice letter of yours that did it.'

'What a charming room you've given us,' Irene said. She smiled and then raised her eyes to gaze at the rough beams set in the ceiling over two hundred years ago. 'I love this house.'

The dinner table was small and brought the three of them close together in an intimate circle. Stoke's massive shoulders leaned in and overshadowed the other two and as they turned their heads during conversation they looked into each other's eyes at close range, saw reflected candlelight, and something else they could not identify.

'These people are strangers,' Varley said to himself in amazement, wondering how they could be so simpatico.

A possible explanation sprang into his mind over coffee when the huge wine bottle was empty and he was pouring cognac. What if they were professionals? It was a preposterous premise and had he not been half drunk he would have buried it away. But he *was* nicely drunk, happily drunk for the first time in years, so he said, 'I've just had a fascinating idea. You're going to laugh.'

'What is it?'

'It's more than likely that you aren't really the William Stokes at all. You are American adventurers, a team of con artists if you like, and you wrote that letter simply to gain access to my house, my life, my confidence.' Varley spread his arms to encompass the scene. 'Done it rather well, too, I should say.'

Was he mistaken or did a frown pass between Stoke and his wife? It might have been a trick of the candlelight. The American said, 'But what about my letterhead? It identifies me as William Stoke, Attorney at Law, of Chattanooga, Tennessee. And that happens to be who I am.'

'Easiest job in the world to have a fake letterhead printed up. First thing you'd do on a scheme like this.' Why was he pressing the idea? It might be taken as uncommonly rude unless his guests accepted it as banter. And how could they do that when Varley himself was not sure whether he was serious or not?

But Stoke did laugh. 'The author's mind at work,' he said. 'I guess you've got to see a twist in everything. But why would we go to all this trouble? What's our motive?'

'That's obvious,' Varley said. 'Financial gain. You get me on good terms, find out where I keep my assets, perhaps persuade me to draw out some money or write a large cheque. Then you vanish, discarding the false identity as you go.'

Had anyone spoken at that moment, Varley might not have felt the hint of danger. But there was silence and he did feel it, a deep thrum like the dong when a tuning fork is struck. It caught him in the chest and buzzed there for seconds, gradually fading away and leaving him feeling cold. He glanced at Stoke, looking for confirmation of the threat, but the big man was tipping back his cognac, lowering the glass and shaking his head, his mouth pursed with amusement.

They sat up till midnight, talking by the fire. The Americans shared the telling of stories about motor trips to New Orleans, to Atlanta, even as far away as California. These distances seemed interstellar to the Englishman who considered the fifty miles to Brighton a long haul.

The visitors acted like a drug on Varley and he found himself opening up about his life, a thing he seldom did. Perhaps the lawyer's subtle questioning led him – he only realised this later; but at the time he rambled on about his solitary state in the world now that he was a widower. No children, no relatives living anywhere; he was a man who could fall off the edge of the earth and never be missed.

'How did your wife …?' Irene began.

Stoke cleared his throat but Varley said, 'No, it's all right. An accident. She struck her head while bathing and drowned.'

Hours later, waking in darkness, Varley sensed movement on the stairs outside his bedroom door. He got up, stepped into slippers, pulled on a robe, and went out quietly onto the landing. He had left the bathroom light burning for his guests' convenience. It illuminated the stairs to the angle where they turned five steps below. Silence. But a fragrance in the air – a woman's scent. It was some time since Varley had experienced this sensation in his house late at night.

He crept down the stairs into a chilly hallway, found the front door standing open, and passed through it onto the flagstone entrance to the narrow garden running along that side of the cottage. Irene Stoke was standing halfway down the path dressed in a long robe. Her braid was undone, the hair brushed out to shoulder width and halfway down her back. He approached her and they stood together in silence. Then she said, 'I couldn't sleep. I'm sorry.'

'It's all right.'

The moon was full. Its pale illumination flooded the brick wall beside them almost like stage lighting. Not yet in leaf, the dormant vine creeping over the wall seemed a dead thing. Varley could smell moist earth and a flood of ozone from the nearby forest. It occurred to him that he ought to spend a couple of hours outside on every night as fine as this one.

Now the woman put a hand on his shoulder in the sort of companionable contact practised by old friends. She leaned forward and kissed him, a touch as cool and fragrant as if she had brushed his cheek with a rose.

'Oughtn't to do that,' Varley said.

She turned her head and looked up at the silhouette of tiled roof and chimneypots with the white, pocked globe of the moon suspended over it. He saw her mouth form a self-deprecating smile as she said with a note of finality, 'I love this house.'

After breakfast Varley found himself alone with William

Stoke. Irene had insisted on going around to the shops to bring back some food. Stoke toyed with his third cup of coffee. 'I guess Irene made a nuisance of herself last night,' he said. 'Sorry about that.'

Having done nothing, Varley felt guilty. 'No trouble at all. Difficult to sleep in strange surroundings.'

But the American was intent on saying more. 'I never expected to tell you this bit of background. But then, I never thought I'd be spending the night in your home.' He went on to explain that this was not a holiday trip. The Stokes were preparing to move to England – under some duress. It seemed Irene had been stealing from department stores for years. She had been in police hands more than once and it had reached the point where Stoke's legal influence was wearing thin. They were talking about putting her away.

'Kleptomania,' Varley said. 'Surely she ought to be seeing a psychiatrist.'

'We've tried that. Some people don't respond very well to analysis. Irene is one of them.' The American gave his host a troubled smile. 'No, I think the only answer is a complete change of scene. Perhaps a small town, a village even, where there's less opportunity for her.'

'But how will you practise law?'

'Fortunately we've done well enough. Money is no problem.'

The front door closed and Irene came through into the kitchen depositing a laden shopping basket on the counter. She sensed the atmosphere in the room. 'My husband has been talking, has he?' Her voice was ultra-cheerful. 'That's

Billy's big problem. He never knows when to shut up.'
Briskly she began unloading the basket.

It was William Stoke's suggestion that they get into the
rented sedan and drive down to the south coast. The weather
was pleasant enough, the warmest March day on record. As
they set out, Stoke said, 'We may even see a village we might
like to settle in.' The truth was now in the open, though
nothing more was said.

They took the Brighton road, then bore east through
Sussex, touching the coast at Hastings where they got out
of the car and walked along the beach for half a mile. Then
on past Winchelsea, New Romney, Dymchurch and Hythe,
and thence along the cliffs towards Folkestone and Dover.

'Not too keen on these areas ahead,' Stoke said. 'Too
metropolitan.'

'Sandgate is a nice little place,' Varley suggested.

Then Irene Stoke said in a bitter tone, 'Or we could pitch
a tent in a field. Or how about a small cabin, of clay and
wattles made.'

Varley realised how serious Stoke was when the man
stopped by a real estate office and went in to find out what
was for sale and for how much. Irene refused to accompany
him, so Varley waited with her in the car. They were silent
for a few minutes. From his place in the back seat he had a
view of her shoulders and the shiny back of her head, the
dark hair tightly braided. The interior of the car smelled
of leather and paint. Finally Irene turned around and said
brightly, 'He's taken you in completely.'

'How do you mean?'

'You believe he's what he says he is.'

'I'm still not with you.'

She closed her eyes while she said, 'You were perceptive last night. Don't be dull now.' She opened her eyes and stared at him. 'Don't you see? Your writer's instinct was correct. He is *not* William Stoke. I am not his wife. This *is* a confidence trick to relieve you of a lot of money.'

'But last night I was only joking.' As he said this, he remembered his uncertainty at the time as to whether he was joking or not. And he recalled the hint of danger that came to him from somewhere across the table.

'Joke or not, you had it right. Ted – that's his real name – got this idea and he's been crafty enough to follow it through. It was all as you said, even to having the letterhead printed.'

Carter Varley felt the sting behind his eyes, called it pure anger, but was not ready to admit he could weep with disappointment at this betrayal. 'Then I'll just have a word with your Ted when he comes back. What's this house hunt, then? Part of the window dressing?'

'Yes. He lives a part one hundred per cent.'

'But why the story about your kleptomania? Is that true?'

'Of course not. It's all designed to lull you, to make you feel sorry for us.' She reached across the seatback and took Varley's hand. 'But be careful. Don't say anything to let him know I've told you. He's a psychopath and you'd be in real danger. Just watch him and say nothing.'

'Why are you telling me this? It can't be in your interest.'

'No. But I think you're a good man.' She squeezed his hand and let it go. 'Protect yourself and I'll take Ted away tomorrow.'

The man who said he was William Stoke came back from

the real estate agent's office with a handful of data sheets on homes for sale. These were passed around and discussed while he drove on. After half an hour the road climbed to a headland with a vast ocean horizon spread out below a high chalk cliff.

'Now there's a view,' Stoke said, pulling the car onto a grassy verge. 'How'd you like to live with that outside your bedroom window?'

Irene was the first one out of the car, running to the very lip of the cliff where she stood with fists on hips, owning everything the eye could see.

'Not too close,' Stoke called. 'It's a lovely fall, but the last couple of feet are murder.'

They studied the view from every direction and began to feel the spank of sun and wind on their cheeks. Then Irene noticed a coffee wagon parked far down the slope by the edge of the highway where a cluster of construction huts bordered a building site.

'That's what we need,' she said. 'Hot coffee.'

Varley insisted on going to get three cups. As he walked down the hill, he wondered what he ought to do about the dangerous situation he was in. Morally, he should call the police. If the pseudo-Stoke character was as bad as Irene said he was, then he deserved to be locked up. But it would be a tricky procedure to approach a policeman. No crime had been committed. There would be no reason to hold him. But once the American knew Varley had become suspicious, he might be capable of anything.

Trudging back up the slope with three coffee cartons in a perforated tray, Varley decided to keep silent and ease the strangers out of his house tomorrow. Once alone, he could consider putting the police on their track.

He was crossing the low mound that prevented a person farther down the hill from seeing anyone on the promontory when he heard Irene calling and saw the struggle taking place near the edge of the cliff. Stoke had Irene by the arms but she was fighting hard, out of her shoes, tearing one arm loose and swinging the free hand in a wide arc against the side of his head. It looked like a slap but it was more; she was holding a rock in that hand. Stoke's knees buckled and he sank to the grass.

'He knows that you know,' she gasped as Varley ran up and set the coffee aside.

'You told him?'

'He suspected. He hurt me.' She showed crimson marks on a pale arm. 'I had to tell him.'

Carter Varley knelt to look at the ugly wound on the man's head. He was moaning, barely conscious. 'You could have killed him.'

'I had to act. He was going to throw you over the cliff as soon as you got back.' Irene reached out to turn Varley's head so that his eyes met hers. They were wide with shock. 'I told you, he's mad.'

When Stoke tried to raise his head, Varley whispered, 'What do we do?'

'We've got to finish him. No, don't think about it. If he comes round, he'll go crazy. We'll never be able to handle him. If we run away, he'll come back to the house. If you call the police, he'll stay out of sight, but you'll never be safe. Believe me, I know him.'

'But what—?'

'Over the edge. Quickly. We'll both say he fell. The head wound will be part of the fall.'

'I can't do that.'

But Irene had Stoke by the arm, his torso half off the ground. She was surprisingly strong. 'Take my word,' she gasped. 'He deserves to die. The things he's done to so many people. You'll be serving justice.'

Stoke's bloodied head was coming up, the whites of his eyes showing, his mouth hanging open. It was a terrifying sight and suddenly Varley wanted an end to it. His heart pounding, he seized the other arm and, together, he and Irene walked the man to the cliff edge. Two steps away they let him go and he tottered forward, stepped crazily into space, and was gone.

The first thing was to wipe away a few traces of blood from the grass, the next to drive to the nearest town for the police. It took some time but by sundown the accident was confirmed, William Stoke was well and truly dead, and Carter Varley was at the wheel of the car driving home.

Irene turned on the radio to a commercial music station. This seemed wrong, so he snapped it off.

'Well!' she said petulantly.

Something else was wrong. 'His papers all tallied with the identification of William Stoke from Chattanooga,' Varley said. 'Driver's licence, social security card, and so on. If he wasn't Stoke, and this was a temporary con game, why had he gone to all that trouble?'

'That's easy. Because he *was* William Stoke. Everything he told you was true. I'm the one who has been lying.'

Varley's creative imagination prevented him from being too surprised. He remembered the hint of danger at the dinner table last night and understood why Stoke had appeared oblivious. The hint of danger had come from Irene.

'Why have you done this?' he asked.

'Because he made my life a hell. He kept sending me to psychiatrists and now he was trying to bury me in some remote village. Away from temptation.' She said this last word contemptuously. 'That's a laugh.'

'Then you've just murdered your husband.'

'*We've* murdered him,' she said. 'Never forget that. I could tell a story to the authorities that would put us both away for a long time. I hope there'll never be a need.'

Varley drove on in outraged, frightened silence. The next time Irene spoke was when he parked the car outside the cottage and went to unlock the front door. She took the key from his hand and turned it in the lock. 'I love this house,' she said.

That night and the next one had their compensations. Varley had almost forgotten what it was to have a woman in his bed. But still he was shocked by the recent events and deeply angry at the way she had manipulated him. He felt she could not be allowed to get away with it. His mind was made up for him when he went into the market a couple of days later and was approached by the manager holding a slip of paper.

'Sorry to trouble you, Mr Varley, but the American lady, staying with you I understand, took a few items and forgot to check them through. Only a small amount, but I thought you'd want me to mention it.'

Varley paid and walked home, his chest rising and falling. He went upstairs and sat at his desk, looking out of the window, thinking. The fine weather had changed and a more seasonal cold wind was blowing across the common.

Yes, he would have to take care of her. A simple household accident was the best way. But not the fall in the bath and the drowning that had done for poor Beatrice. This would have to be something else, perhaps a broken neck at the bottom of those twisting stairs. They were dangerous till you got used to them.

The office door opened and Irene came in without knocking. She was carrying a glass of whisky – he frowned at his watch – at eleven in the morning. 'What are you up to all alone in here?' she asked, sounding bright and self-satisfied.

Carter Varley picked up a pen and added a few words to a paragraph of recent scrawl. 'Oh, just busy with my plotting,' he said.

It was her second drink, so Irene did not catch the hint of danger in his voice.

An Exciting Christmas Eve

Arthur Conan Doyle

It has often seemed to me to be a very strange and curious thing that danger and trouble should follow those who are most anxious to lead a quiet and uneventful life. I myself have been such a one, and I find on looking back that it was in those very periods of my existence which might have been most confidently reckoned on as peaceful that some unexpected adventure has befallen me, like the thunderbolt from an unclouded sky which shook the nerves of old Horace. Possibly my experience differs from that of other men, and I may have been especially unfortunate. If so, there is the more reason why I should mourn over my exceptional lot, and record it for the benefit of those more happily circumstanced.

Just compare my life with that of Leopold Walderich, and you will see what I complain of. We both come from Mulhausen, in Baden, and that is why I single him out as an example, though many others would do as well. He was a man who professed to be fond of adventure. Now listen to what occurred. We went to Heidelberg University together. I was quiet, studious, and unassuming; he was impetuous, reckless, and idle. For three years he revelled in every sort of riot, while I frequented the laboratories, and rarely deserted my books save for a hurried walk into the country when a pain in my head and ringing in my ears warned me that I was trifling with my constitution.

Yet during that period his life was comparatively uneventful, while my whole existence was a series of hairbreadth perils and escapes. I damaged my eyesight and nearly choked myself by the evolution of a poisonous gas. I swallowed a trichina in my ham, and was prostrated for weeks. I was hurled out of a second-floor window by an English lunatic because I ventured to quote the solemn and serious passage in Schoppheim's *Weltgeschichte* which proves Waterloo to have been a purely Prussian victory, and throws grave doubts on the presence of any British force nearer than Brussels! Twice I was nearly drowned, and once I should have been precipitated from the parapet of the schloss but for the assistance of this same Englishman. These are a few of the incidents which occurred to me while endeavouring to read in seclusion for my degree.

Even in smaller matters this luck of mine held good. I can well remember, for example, that on one occasion the wilder spirits of the Badischer Corps ventured upon an unusually hare-brained escapade. There was a farmer about a couple of miles from the town whose name was Nicholas Bodeck. This man had made himself obnoxious to the students, and they determined to play a prank upon him in return. An enormous number of little caps were accordingly made with the colours of the Corps upon them, and the conspirators invaded his premises in the middle of the night and gummed them upon the heads of all the fowls.

They certainly had a very comical effect, as I had an opportunity of judging, for I happened to pass that way in the morning. I supposed that Walderich and his friends carried out their little joke for excitement, knowing the farmer to be a resolute man. They got no excitement from it, however; it was I who got that. Activity was never my strong point, but certainly I ran those two miles that morning with incredible speed – and so did the five men with pitchforks who ran behind me!

These things may seem trivial, but, as you say in England, a straw shows which way the wind blows, and these were only indications of what was to come.

I took my degree in medicine, and found myself Herr Doctor Otto von Spee. I then graduated in science, receiving much applause for my thesis, 'On the Explosive Compounds of the Tri-methyl Series'. I was quoted as an authority in works of science, and my professors prophesied that a great career lay before me. My studies, however, were suddenly put an end to by the outbreak of the great war with France.

Walderich volunteered into one of the crack regiments, fought in nearly every engagement, covered himself with glory, and came back unhurt to be decorated with the cross for valour. I was stationed in an ambulance which never even crossed the frontier, yet I succeeded in breaking my arm by tumbling over a stretcher, and in contracting erysipelas from one of the few wounds which came under my care. I got no medal or cross, and went back quietly to Berlin after it was all over, and there I settled as privat docent of chemistry and physics.

You will naturally ask what all this has to do with my Christmas story. You shall see in time that it is necessary I should tell you this, in order that you may appreciate that crowning event in my long list of misfortunes. You must remember also that I am a German and therefore somewhat long-winded perhaps, as my nation has the reputation of being. I have often admired the dashing, rattling manner of English storytellers, but I fear if I were to attempt to imitate this it would be as if one of our own ponderous old Mulhausen storks were to adopt the pretty, graceful airs of your Christmas robins. You shall hear in time all that I have to say about my Christmas Eve.

After I had settled in Berlin I endeavoured to combine the private practice of medicine with my labours as a privat docent, which corresponds to what you call a 'coach' in England. For some years I pursued this plan, but I found that my practice, being largely among the lower classes, favoured my unfortunate propensity for getting into trouble, and I determined to abandon it.

I took a secluded house, therefore, in a quiet quarter of the city, and there I gave myself up to scientific research, pursuing principally the same train of investigation which had originally attracted me – namely, the chemistry of explosive compounds.

My expenses were small, and all the money which I could spare was laid out on scientific instruments and mechanical contrivances of different sorts. Soon I had a snug little laboratory which, if not as pretentious as that at Heidelberg, was quite as well fitted to supply my wants. It is true that the neighbours grumbled, and that Gretchen, my housekeeper, had to be quieted with a five-mark piece, after having been blown up three separate times, and blown down once while engaged in fixing an electric wire upon the summit of an outhouse. These little matters, however, were easily settled, and I found my life rapidly assuming a peaceful complexion, of which I had long despaired.

I was happy – and what is more I was becoming famous. My 'Remarks on Cacodyl' in the *Monthly Archives of Science* created no small sensation, and Herr Raubenthal of Bonn characterised them as '*meisterlich*', though dissenting from many of my deductions. I was enabled, however, in a later contribution to the same journal to recount certain experiments which were sufficient to convince that eminent savant that my view of the matter was the correct one.

After this victory I was universally recognised as an authority in my own special branch, and as one of the foremost living workers at explosives. The government appointed me to the torpedo commission at Kiel, and many other honours were bestowed upon me. One of the consequences of this sudden accession of celebrity was that I found myself in great request as a lecturer, both at scientific gatherings and at those meetings for the education of the people which have become so common in the metropolis. By these means my name got into the daily papers as one learned in such matters, and to this it is that I ascribe the events which I am about to narrate.

It was a raw windy Christmas Eve. The sleet pattered

against the windowpanes, and the blast howled among the skeleton branches of the gaunt poplar trees in my garden. There were few people in the street, and those few had their coats buttoned up, and their chins upon their breasts, and hurried rapidly homewards, staggering along against the force of the storm. Even the big policeman outside had ceased to clank up and down, and was crouching in a doorway for protection.

Many a lonely man might have felt uncomfortable upon such a night, but I was too interested in my work to have time for any sympathy with the state of the weather. A submarine mine was engaging my attention, and in a leaden tank in front of me I had stuck a small pellet of my new explosive. The problem was how far its destructive capacities would be modified by the action of the water. The matter was too important to allow me to feel despondent. Besides, one of Gretchen's lovers was in the kitchen, and his gruff expressions of satisfaction, whether with her charms or my beer, or both, were sufficiently audible to banish any suspicion of loneliness.

I was raising my battery onto the table, and was connecting the wires carefully so as to explode the charge, when I heard a short, quick step outside the window, and immediately afterwards a loud knock at the outer door.

Now I very seldom had a call from any of my limited number of acquaintances, and certainly never upon such a night as this. I was astonished for a moment; then concluding that it was a visitor of Gretchen's, I continued to work at my apparatus.

To my very great surprise, after Gretchen had opened the

door there was some muttering in the hall, and then a quiet tap at the entrance of my sanctum, followed by the appearance of a tall lady whom I could vow that I had never seen in my life before.

Her face was covered by a thick dark veil, and her dress was of the same sombre colour, so that I concluded her to be a widow. She walked in with a decisive energetic step, and after glancing round, seated herself quietly upon the sofa between the voltaic pile and my stand of reagents – all this without saying a word, or apparently taking the slightest notice of my presence.

'Good evening, madam,' I remarked, when I had somehow recovered my composure.

'Would you do me a favour, doctor?' she replied, brusquely, in a harsh voice, which harmonised with her gaunt angular figure.

'Surely, madam,' I answered, in my most elegant manner. I remember a girl at Heidelberg used to say that I had a very fascinating way sometimes. Of course it was only a joke, but still something must have put it into her head or she would never have said it. 'What can I do for you?' I asked.

'You can send away that servant of yours, who is listening at the door.'

At this moment, before I could move hand or foot, there were a succession of tremendous bumps, followed by a terrible crash and a prolonged scream. It was evident that my unhappy domestic had fallen downstairs in her attempt to avoid detection. I was about to rise, but the stranger arrested me.

'Never mind now,' she said. 'We can proceed to business.'

I bowed my head to show that I was all attention.

'The fact is, doctor,' she continued, 'that I wish you to come back with me and give me your opinion upon a case.'

'My dear madam,' I answered, 'I have long retired from the practice of my profession. If you go down the street, however, you will see the surgery of Doctor Benger, who is a most competent man, and who will be happy to accompany you.'

'No, no,' cried my companion, in great distress. 'You or no one! You or no one! My poor dear husband cried out as I left him that Otto von Spee was the only man who could bring him back from the tomb. They will all be broken-hearted if I return without you. Besides, the professors at the hospital said that you were the only one in Europe who would be capable of dealing with it.'

Now, devoted as I was to scientific research, I had always had a conviction in my mind that I had the makings in me of a first-class practical physician. It was inexpressibly consoling to hear that the heads of the profession had endorsed this opinion by referring a curious case to my judgement. The more I thought of it, however, the more extraordinary did it seem. 'Are you sure?' I asked.

'Oh yes, quite sure.'

'But I am a specialist – a student of explosives. I have had very little experience in practice. What is the matter with your husband?'

'He has a tumour.'

'A tumour? I know nothing of tumours.'

'Oh come, dear Doctor von Spee; come and look at it!' implored the female, producing a handkerchief from her pocket and beginning to sob convulsively.

It was too much. I had lived a secluded life, and had never before seen a female in distress.

'Madam,' I said, 'I shall be happy to accompany you.'

I regretted that promise the moment it was uttered. There was a wild howl of wind in the chimney which reminded me of the inclemency of the night. However, my word was pledged, and there was no possibility of escape. I left the room with as cheerful an aspect as possible, while Gretchen wrapped a shawl round my neck and muffled me up to the best of her ability.

What could there be about this tumour, I wondered, which had induced the learned surgeons to refer it to my judgement – I who was rather an artillerist than a physician? Could it be that the growth was of such stony hardness that no knife could remove it, and that explosives were necessary for extraction? The idea was so comical that I could scarce refrain from laughing.

'Now, madam,' I said re-entering the study, 'I am at your disposal.' As I spoke I knocked against the electric machine, causing a slight transmission of the current along the wires, so that the submarine mine exploded with a crash, blowing a little column of water into the air. Accustomed as I was to such accidents, I confess that I was considerably startled by the suddenness of the occurrence. My companion, however, sat perfectly impassive upon the sofa, and then rose without the slightest sign of surprise or emotion, and walked out of the room.

'She has the nerves of a grenadier,' I mentally ejaculated, as I followed her into the street.

'Is it far?' I asked, as we started off through the storm.

'Not very far,' she answered; 'and I took the liberty of bringing a cab for you, for fear Herr Doctor might catch cold. Ah, here it comes.'

As she spoke, a closed carriage dashed along the road, and pulled up beside us.

'Have you got Otto von Spee?' asked a sallow-faced man, letting down the window and protruding his head.

'Yes, here he is.'

'Then shove him in.'

For the moment I was inclined to regard the expression as a playful figure of speech, but my companion soon dispelled the delusion by seizing me by the collar and hurling me, with what seemed superhuman strength, into the vehicle. I fell upon the floor, and was dragged on to a seat by the man, while the other sprang in, slammed the door, and the horses dashed off at a furious gallop.

I lay back in a state of bewilderment, hardly able to realise what had occurred. It was pitch dark inside the carriage, but I could hear my two companions conversing in low whispers. Once I attempted to expostulate and demand an explanation of their conduct, but a threatening growl, and a rough hand placed over my mouth, warned me to be silent. I was neither a wealthy man nor particularly well connected, nor was I a politician. What then, could be the object of these people in kidnapping me in such an elaborate fashion? The more I pondered over it, the more mysterious did it seem.

Once we halted for a moment, and a third man got into the carriage, who also enquired anxiously whether Otto von Spee had been secured, and expressed his satisfaction on being answered in the affirmative. After this stoppage we rattled along even more quickly than before, the vehicle rocking from side to side with the velocity, and the clatter of the horses' hoofs sounding above the howling of the gale. It seemed to me that we must have passed through every street in Berlin before, with a sudden jar, the coachman pulled up, and my captors intimated that I was to descend.

I had hardly time to look about me and realise the fact that I was in a narrow street in some low quarter of the city. A door opened in front of us, and the two men led me through it, while the herculean female followed us, effectually cutting off any hopes of escape.

We were in a long passage or corridor, feebly illuminated by a couple of flickering lamps, whose yellow glare seemed to intensify the darkness around them. After walking about twenty metres or more we came to a massive door, blocking our passage. One of my guardians struck it a blow with a stick which he carried in his hand, when it reverberated with a metallic clang, and swung open, closing with a snap behind us.

At this point I ventured to stop and expostulate with my companions once again. My only answer, however, was a shove from the individual behind me, which shot me through a half-opened door into a comfortable little chamber beyond. My captors followed in a more leisurely manner, and after turning the lock, they proceeded to seat themselves, motioning to me that I should do the same.

The room in which I found myself was small but elegantly furnished. A fire was sparkling in the grate, and the bright colours of the handsome suite of furniture and variegated carpet helped to give it a cheering aspect. The pictures on the walls, however, went far towards neutralising this effect. They were very numerous, but every one of them treated of some unpleasant or murderous passage of history. Many of them were so distant that I was unable to decipher the inscriptions. To a scholar like myself, however, the majority were able to tell their own story. There was the lunatic Schtaps in the garden, making his attempt upon the life of the First Napoleon. Above it was a sketch of Orsini with his cowardly bomb, waiting silently among the loungers at the opera. A statuette of Ravaillac was placed upon a pedestal in the corner, while a large oil painting of the strangling of the unhappy Emperor Paul in his bedchamber occupied the whole of one wall of the apartment.

These things did not tend to raise my spirits, and the appearance of my three companions was still less calculated to do so. I had several times doubted the sex of the individual who had seduced me from my comfortable home, but the veil had now been removed and revealed a dark moustache and sunburnt countenance, with a pair of searching, sinister eyes, which seemed to look into my very soul. Of the others, one was gaunt and cadaverous, the other insignificant-looking, with a straggling beard and unhealthy complexion.

'We are very sorry, Doctor von Spee, to be reduced to this necessity,' said the last-mentioned individual, 'but unhappily we had no other method of securing the pleasure of your society.'

I bowed – a little sulkily, I am afraid.

'I must apologise for any little liberties I have taken, above all for having deprived you of the satisfaction of beholding my husband's remarkable tumour,' said my original acquaintance.

I thought of the manner in which he had bundled me about like an empty portmanteau, and my bow was even more sulky than before.

'I trust, gentlemen,' I remarked, 'that since your practical joke has been so admirably carried out, you will now permit me to return to the studies which you have interrupted.'

'Not so fast, Herr Doctor – not so fast,' said the tall man, rising to his feet. 'We have a little duty which you shall perform before you leave us. It is nothing more nor less than to give a few enquirers into the truth a lesson upon your own special subject. Might I beg you to step in this direction?'

He walked over to a side door, painted of the same colour as the paper on the wall, and held it persuasively open. Resistance was useless, as the other confederates had also risen, and were standing on either side of me. I yielded to circumstances, and walked out as directed.

We passed down a second passage, rather shorter than the first, and much more brilliantly illuminated. At the end of it a heavy velvet curtain was hung, which covered a green baize folding door. This was swung open, and I found myself, to my astonishment, in a large room in which a considerable number of people were assembled. They were arranged in long rows, and sat so as to face a raised platform at one end of the apartment, on which was a single chair, with a small round table, littered with a number of objects.

My companions ushered me in, and our entrance was greeted with considerable applause. It was clear that we had been awaited, for there was a general movement of expectation throughout the assembly. Glancing round, I could see that the majority of the company were dressed as artisans or labourers. There were some, however, who were respectably and even fashionably attired, and a few whose blue coats and gilt shoulder bands proclaimed them to be officers in the army. Their nationalities seemed almost as varied as their occupations. I could distinguish the dolichocephalic head of the Teuton, the round, curl-covered cranium of the Celt, and the prognathous jaw and savage features of the Slav. I could almost have imagined myself looking into one of the cabinets of casts in my friend Landerstein's anthropological museum.

However, I had not much time for wonder or reflection. One of my guardians led me across the room, and I found myself standing at the table, which I have already mentioned as being situated upon a raised dais. My appearance in this situation was the signal for a fresh outburst of applause, which, with clapping of hands and drumming of sticks upon the floor, lasted for some considerable time.

When it had subsided, the gaunt man who had come with me in the carriage walked up to the dais and addressed a few words to the audience. 'Gentlemen,' he said, 'you will perceive that the committee have succeeded in keeping their promise of bringing the celebrated' – 'berühmte' was the word he used – 'Doctor Otto von Spee to address you.' Here there was renewed applause.

'Doctor,' he continued, turning to me, 'I think a few words of public explanation will not be amiss in this matter. You are well known as an authority upon explosives. Now, all these gentlemen and myself have an interest in this subject, and would gladly listen to your views upon it. We are particularly anxious that you should give us clear and precise directions as to the method of preparing dynamite, guncotton and other such substances, as we sometimes have a little difficulty in obtaining such things for our experiments. You shall also tell us about the effect of temperature, water and other agents upon these substances, the best method of storing them, and the way of using them to the greatest advantage. For our part, we shall listen attentively and treat you well, always provided that you make no attempt to summon aid or to escape. Should you be so ill-advised as to do either' — here he slapped his pocket — 'you shall become as intimately acquainted with projectiles as you now are with explosives.' I cannot say that this struck me as a good joke, but it seemed to meet considerable favour among the audience.

'I wish to add a few words to the remarks of our learned president,' said a small man, rising up from among the first line of the company. 'I have placed upon the table such materials as I could lay my hands upon in order that the learned doctor may be able to illustrate his discourse by any experiments which he may think appropriate. I may warn him, in conclusion, to speak somewhat slowly and distinctly, as some of his hearers are but imperfectly acquainted with the German language.'

Here was my old luck again with a vengeance! At a time when Walderich and every gay dog in Berlin were snoring peacefully in their beds, I — I, Doctor Otto von Spee, the modest man of science — was lecturing to a murderous secret organisation — for my audience could be nothing else — and teaching them to forge the weapons with which they were to attack society and everything which should be treasured and revered. And on such a night as this too! Should I, then, put it in their power to convert a house into an arsenal, to destroy the stability of the Fatherland, and even perhaps attempt the life of my beloved Kaiser? Never! I swore it – never!

Most small men who wear spectacles are obstinate. I am a small man with spectacles, and I was no exception to the rule. I clenched my teeth, and felt that *ruat caelum*, never a word should pass my lips that might be of any help to them. I should not refuse to lecture, but I was determined to avoid those very points upon which they desired to be instructed.

I was not allowed much time for meditation. An ominous murmur among the audience, and a shuffling of feet upon the floor, betokened their impatience. I must say, however, that many of them seemed actuated with rather kindly feelings towards me, more particularly one stoutish individual of a well-marked Celtic type, who, not content with smiling all over his florid countenance, waved his arms occasionally in motions intended to indicate sympathy and inspire confidence.

I stepped up to the table, which was covered all over with such objects as were thought to have a bearing upon my subject. Some of them were rather curious – a lump of salt, an iron teapot, part of the broken axle of a wheel, and a large pair of kitchen bellows. Others were more appropriate. There was a piece of guncotton which could not have weighed less than a couple of pounds, coarse cotton, starch, various acids, a Bunsen burner, tubes of fulminate of mercury, some dynamite powder and a large pitcher of water. There was also a carafe and tumbler for my own use, should I feel so disposed.

'*Meine herren*,' I began, with perhaps a slight quaver in my voice, 'we have met here tonight for the purpose of studying dynamite and other explosives.' It flowed naturally from my lips, as it was the stereotyped formula with which my discourses at the Educationische Institut were usually commenced. My audience seemed, however, to be much amused, and the florid Celt was convulsed with admiration and merriment. Even the forbidding-looking man who had been referred to as the president condescended to smile his approval and remark that I adapted myself readily to my circumstances.

'These substances,' I continued, 'are powerful agents either for good or for evil. For good when used for the quarrying of rocks, the removal of impediments to navigation, or the destruction of houses during a conflagration. For evil—'

'I think you had better pass on to something more practical,' said the president, grimly.

'On dipping starch into certain liquids,' I resumed, 'it is found to assume an explosive property. The attention of a learned countryman of ours, the chemist Schonbein, was directed to the fact, and he found that by treating cotton in a similar manner the effect was enormously increased. Schonbein was a man respected among his contemporaries, devoted to his country, and loyal—'

'Pass on!' said the president.

'After being treated in this fashion,' I continued, 'the cotton is found to gain eighty per cent in weight. This substance is more susceptible to an increase of temperature than gunpowder, igniting at $300°$ Fahrenheit, while the latter requires a heat of $560°$ for its explosion. Guncotton can also

ARTHUR CONAN DOYLE

be exploded by a blow, which is not the case with a mixture of carbon, sulphur and saltpetre.'

Here there were some angry murmurs among the company, and the president interrupted me for the third time.

'These gentlemen complain,' he said, 'that you have left no definite impression upon their minds as to how the substance is manufactured. Perhaps you will kindly dwell more fully upon the point.'

'I have no further remarks to make,' I said.

There was another threatening murmur, and the president took something out of the pocket of his coat, and toyed with it negligently. 'I think you had better reconsider your decision,' he remarked.

Most little men with spectacles are timid. Again I was no exception to the rule. I am ashamed to say that the peril of my Fatherland and even of my Kaiser suddenly vanished from my recollection. I only realised that I, Otto von Spee, was standing upon the brink of eternity. After all, I argued, they could find out for themselves in any book upon chemistry. Why should my valuable life be sacrificed for such a trifle? I resumed my lecture with somewhat undignified haste.

'Guncotton is manufactured by steeping cotton waste in nitric acid. The explosion is caused by the oxygen of the acid combining with the carbon of the wool. It should be well cleaned with water after manufacture, otherwise the superfluous nitric acid acts directly upon the wool, charring it and gradually reducing it to a gummy mass. During this process heat is often evolved sufficient to explode the cotton, so that it is a dangerous matter to neglect the cleaning. After this a little sulphuric acid may be used to get rid of the moisture, when the substance is ready for use.'

There was considerable applause at this point of my discourse, several of the audience taking notes of my remarks.

While I had been speaking I had been making a careful survey of the room in the hope of seeing some possibility of escape. The dais upon which I stood extended as far as the side wall, in which there was a window. The window was half open, and, could I reach it, there appeared to be a deserted-looking garden outside, which might communicate with the street. No one could intercept me before I reached the window, but then there was the deadly weapon with which my cadaverous acquaintance was still trifling. He was sitting on the other side, and the table would partially protect me should I venture upon a dash. Could I screw up my courage to make an attempt? Not yet, at any rate.

'General von Link,' I continued, 'the Austrian artillerist, is one of our leading authorities upon guncotton. He experimented upon it in field-pieces, but—'

'Never mind that,' said the president.

'After being manufactured, guncotton may be compressed under water. When compressed it is perfectly safe, and cannot be discharged. This sample which we have upon the table is not compressed. No amount of heat will have any effect upon the wet cotton. In an experiment tried in England a storehouse containing guncotton was burned down without there being any explosion. If, however, a charge of fulminated mercury, or a small piece of dry cotton, be fired in connection with a damp disc, it will be sufficient to discharge it. I shall now proceed to demonstrate this to you by an experiment.'

An idea had come into my mind. Upon the table there was lying a mixture of sugar and chlorate of potash, used with sulphuric acid as a fuse for mining purposes. A bottle of the acid was also ready to my hand. I knew the white dense cloud of smoke which is raised by the imperfect combustion of these bodies. Could I make it serve as a screen between the weapon of the president and myself?

For a moment the plan seemed wild and unfeasible; still, it offered some chance of escape, and the more I thought it over the more reconciled I became to it. Of course, even after getting through the window there was the possibility that the garden might prove to be a cul-de-sac, and that my pursuers might overtake me. But then, on the other hand, I had no guarantee that I might not be murdered at the conclusion of my lecture. From what I knew of the habits of such men I considered it to be extremely probable. It was better to risk – but no, I would not think of what I was risking.

'I am now going to show you the effect of fulminate of mercury upon a small piece of damp cotton,' I said, shaking out the sugar and chlorate of potash upon the edge of the table and pushing the large piece of cotton to the other end to be out of danger from the effects of the explosion.

'You will observe that the fact of the substance having been soaked with water does not in any way hinder its action.' Here I poured the sulphuric acid over the mixture, dropped the bottle, and fled for the window amid a perfect cloud of smoke.

Most little men with spectacles are not remarkable for

activity. Ha! there at last I proved myself to be an exception. I seemed hardly to put my foot to the ground between leaving the table and shooting out through the window as the equestrians fly through hoops in the circus. I was well outside before the sharp crack which I was expecting sounded in the chamber behind me, and then—

Ah! what then? How can I ever hope to describe it? There was a low, deep rumble, which seemed to shake the ground, swelling and swelling in sound until it culminated in a roar which split the very heavens. Flames danced before my eyes, burning wood and stones and debris came clattering down around me, and as I stared about me in bewilderment I received a crushing blow upon the head, and fell.

How long I may have remained unconscious it is difficult to say. Some time, at any rate, for when I came to myself I was stretched upon the bed in my own little chamber at home, while the devoted Gretchen bathed my temples with vinegar and water. In the doorway were standing a couple of stalwart *polizei diener*, who bobbed their helmeted heads and grinned their satisfaction on seeing that I was returning to consciousness.

It was some while before I could recall anything of what had passed. Then gradually came the recollection of my mysterious visitor, of the wild drive through the storm, of the impromptu lecture on dynamite, and lastly of some strange and unaccountable accident. Strange it still remains, but I think that when we reflect that the table was between the bullet and me, and that on that table were two pounds of guncotton liable to ignition at a blow, we have not very far to go for an explanation. I have fired a pistol at a distance into a small piece of the same substance since that occasion with very much the same result.

And where was the house, you will ask, and what was the fate of its inmates? Ah! there my lips are sealed. The police of the Fatherland are active and cunning, and they have commanded me to say nothing – not even to my dearest friend – upon either point. No doubt they have their reasons for it, and I must obey. Perhaps they wish other conspirators to imagine that more has been found out than is actually the case. I may say, however, that it is not conducive to long life or perfect health to be present on such an occasion. That, at least, no one can object to.

I am nearly well again now, thanks to Gretchen and Dr Benger, who lives down the road. I can hobble about, and my neighbours are already beginning to complain of the noxious vapours which I evolve. I fear I have not quite the same enthusiasm, however, upon the subject of explosives as I entertained before my midnight lecture on dynamite. The subject seems to have lost many of its charms. It may be that in the course of time I may return to my first love once again; at present, however, I remain a quiet privat docent of the more elementary branches of chemistry. It is that very quietness which weighs upon my mind. I fear that I am on the verge of some other unexpected adventure. There is one thing, however, upon which I am unalterably determined. Should every relative that I have in the world, with the imperial family and half the population of Berlin, be clamouring at my door for medical advice, I shall never again protrude my head after nightfall. I am content to work away in my own little groove, and have laid aside forever the pretensions to be looked upon as a practical physician which I entertained before that eventful Christmas Eve.

Credits

'The Haunted Crescent' by Peter Lovesey, reprinted by permission of Vannessa Holt

'New Murders for Old' by Carter Dickson, reprinted by permission of David Higham Associates

'A Very Commonplace Murder' by P.D. James, reprinted by permission of Greene and Heaton

'The Hours of Darkness' by Edmund Crispin, reprinted by permission of HarperCollins

'Losing the Plot' by Catherine Aird, reprinted by permission of Aitken Alexander

'The Carpet Bagger' by Colin Dexter, reprinted by permission of Pan Macmillan

While every effort has been made to contact copyright-holders of each story, the editor and publishers would be grateful for information where they have been unable to trace them, and would be glad to make amendments in further editions.